Why on earth was she so nervous?

She'd entertained hundreds of people at the inn. Mattie could coax conversation from the shiest of individuals. She could have the most serious folks laughing and enjoying themselves in a matter of mere moments. Entertaining was her forte. Amusing her guests, diverting them from their regular, workaday lives, was what kept people coming back to her B & B.

Feeding one man dinner shouldn't have her all atwitter like this.

But her night prince wasn't any ordinary man.

Conner Thunder intrigued her. But no matter how attractive she found him, there was something not quite right about his homecoming....

Dear Reader,

In the spirit of Valentine's Day, we have some wonderful stories for you this February from Silhouette Romance to guarantee that every day is filled with love and tenderness.

DeAnna Talcott puts a fresh spin on the tale of Cupid, who finally meets her match in *Cupid Jones Gets Married* (#1646), the latest in the popular SOULMATES series. And Carla Cassidy has been working overtime with her incredibly innovative, incredibly fun duo, *What if I'm Pregnant…?* (#1644) and *If the Stick Turns Pink…* (#1645), about the promise of love a baby could bring to two special couples!

Then Elizabeth Harbison takes us on a fairy-tale adventure in *Princess Takes a Holiday* (#1643). A glamour-weary royal who hides her identity meets the man of her dreams when her car breaks down in a small North Carolina town. In *Dude Ranch Bride* (#1642), Madeline Baker brings us strong, sexy Lakota Ethan Stormwalker, whose ex-flame shows up at his ranch in a wedding gown—without a groom! And in Donna Clayton's *Thunder in the Night* (#1647), the third in THE THUNDER CLAN family saga, a single act of kindness changes Conner Thunder's life forever….

Be sure to come back next month for more emotion-filled love stories from Silhouette Romance. Happy reading!

Mary-Theresa Hussey

Mary-Theresa Hussey
Senior Editor

Please address questions and book requests to:
Silhouette Reader Service
U.S.: 3010 Walden Ave., P.O. Box 1325, Buffalo, NY 14269
Canadian: P.O. Box 609, Fort Erie, Ont. L2A 5X3

Thunder in the Night

Donna Clayton

THE THUNDER CLAN

SILHOUETTE *Romance*®

Published by Silhouette Books

America's Publisher of Contemporary Romance

To Diane Grecco,

for all those smiley faces and hearts in the margins.
But most of all for asking those tough questions
that made this series all it could be.

Thank you!

 SILHOUETTE BOOKS

ISBN 0-373-19647-4

THUNDER IN THE NIGHT

Copyright © 2003 by Donna Fasano

Visit Silhouette at www.eHarlequin.com

Printed in U.S.A.

Books by Donna Clayton

DONNA CLAYTON

is the recipient of the Diamond Author Award for Literary Achievement 2000 as well as two HOLT Medallions. She became a writer through her love of reading. As a child, she marveled at her ability to travel the world, experience swashbuckling adventures and meet amazingly bold and daring people without ever leaving the shade of the huge oak in her very own backyard. She takes great pride in knowing that, through her work, she provides her readers the chance to indulge in some purely selfish romantic entertainment.

One of her favorite pastimes is traveling. Her other interests include walking, reading, visiting with friends, teaching Sunday school, cooking and baking, and she still collects cookbooks, too. In fact, her house is overrun with them.

Please write to Donna c/o Silhouette Books. She'd love to hear from you!

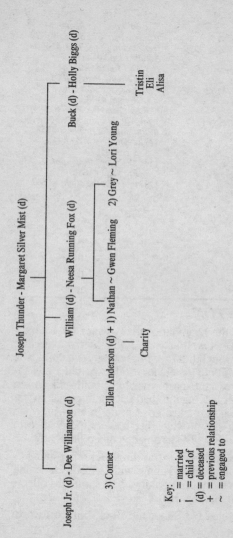

Joseph Thunder - Margaret Silver Mist (d)

Joseph Jr. (d) - Dee Williamson (d)   William (d) - Neesa Running Fox (d)   Buck (d) - Holly Biggs (d)

3) Conner   Ellen Anderson (d) + 1) Nathan ~ Gwen Fleming   2) Grey ~ Lori Young

Charity

Tristin
Eli
Alisa

Key:
- = married
| = child of
(d) = deceased
+ = previous relationship
~ = engaged to

Joseph Thunder is a well-respected shaman of his Kolheek people. But he is a sad man. No one should outlive his child; however, he has outlived all three of his sons and daughters-in-law. He has raised his five grandsons and he's determined to see that his grandchildren live happy and successful lives...something that fate has stolen from Joseph's own sons.

1) Nathan's story: THE SHERIFF'S 6-YEAR-OLD SECRET (RS#1623)
2) Grey's story: THE DOCTOR'S PREGNANT PROPOSAL (RS#1635)
3) Conner's story: THUNDER IN THE NIGHT (RS#1647)

Prologue

With a sharp inhalation, Conner Thunder bolted upright on the mattress, his heart racing like the hooves of a stampeding stallion. Sheer panic seemed to hold sovereignty over his rigid body. His breathing was labored. His muscles bunched. Sweat glistened on his skin, chilling him to the bone.

Quickly the last vestiges of the shadowy dream vaporized into nothingness as if it had been a night specter dissolved by the simple flick of a light switch. One moment it was there in all its terrorizing glory, the next it had vanished without a trace.

He scrubbed his fingers over his face, then combed them straight back over his scalp, his hair swishing across his damp back. Once his pulse settled and his breathing slowed, rational thought returned. The dream was disturbing, yes. But it was just that...a dream. He took a deep breath and let it out in a slow, conscious measure.

Conner flung back the sheet and stood, the wooden plank floor of the cabin smooth against his bare feet. In the kitchen area he turned on the spigot and splashed water over his face, neck and chest. Grabbing a terry towel, he dried himself and then reached for his jeans and sweatshirt. He felt as if the walls were closing in on him. The need to escape welled up sharply.

Donning his worn hide moccasins, he slipped out into the silky night. The cool darkness invigorated his senses and he plunged into the forest with no aim save that of clearing the disturbing images from his head.

He knew what had triggered the reoccurrence of the haunting childhood nightmare. It was the accident. The accident that had left a young man paralyzed for the rest of his life. The accident that should never have happened.

Pine needles grazed his cheek, the pungent scent settling over him as he passed the evergreen that grew by the path. He hadn't been back to Smoke Valley Reservation in years. He'd been too busy, first attending college in Boston and then staying to build what had ultimately turned into a successful business. But the dreams had brought him back.

The sound of water cascading over rocks told him he was very close to Smoke Lake. Although he couldn't yet see the glassy water, he could smell the moisture, see the hazy mist hanging heavy in the air.

The vision that haunted his nights was the same one he'd suffered as a child. He couldn't say at what age the dream had stopped, but he did remember the fear and helplessness he'd felt in his youth. The image was filled with an excruciating heat, animated movement and booming yet muffled voices. Angry voices. Yet the picture was filmy, as if he was seeing it through some kind of shroud.

Conner swiped a hand over weary eyes. Dreams had special meaning to the Kolheek. Until he deciphered the images, they would continue to cause him anguish and sleepless nights. A whispery voice had called him home. Home to Smoke Valley Reservation. Home to his people, his clan, his own kind. Here he would find the means to interpret this eerie, disquieting vision.

Conner stopped short, cocking his head a fraction to listen. Something unusual, something not of the night, was out there.

There it was again.

His brow puckered as he tried to make sense of the low resonance carried on the mists. If he didn't know better he'd say it was…crying. The soft shuddering sobs of…a woman. The soles of his moccasins were silent on the dirt path as he hurried now toward the lakeshore.

The mist turned milky the closer he got to the water, saturating the air around him. But suddenly he was able to make out her form. Concern and resolve had him moving closer.

She was young. Mid-twenties, he guessed. Her blond hair, long and straight, hung down her back, almost glowing gold in the ghostly light that radiated from the fat moon overhead.

Evidently intuition told her she wasn't alone, for she looked up at him. The tears in her eyes tugged at him, drew him to her side like some mysterious, indomitable energy.

Without hesitation he reached out his hand.

Without hesitation her creamy palm slid against his.

The moment her flesh contacted his, Conner's whole being bristled with an awareness that rocked him to his very core. He nearly gasped at the strength of emotion that rolled through his being. With his free hand he cupped her jaw. The sadness in her electric-blue eyes made his heart wrench. He felt her anguish. Suffered it as if it were his own.

Although he wasn't even aware of it, in that instant his own distress—the torment that had sent him rushing out into the night—was totally forgotten and his only focus was to comfort this beautiful stranger.

"Don't cry," he crooned softly, caressing her cheek with the backs of his fingers. "You'll be all right."

Her petite shoulders seemed to relax then, if only a little, and she rested her head against his chest. Her hair was soft against the underside of his jaw. She smelled of warm sun and wildflowers, and Conner's body quickened deep inside.

Swiftly and silently he chastised himself for feeling sensually aroused, but he knew at the same time it wasn't something he could help. He was a normal, red-blooded man. And there was an exquisite woman pressed against him.

Talking, he decided, would take his mind off the lust that surged through him like molten lava.

"Whatever it is," he whispered, "it's going to be okay. I promise you."

It was a silly promise, really. He didn't know her, didn't know what it was that had her upset and crying. All he did know was that he wanted to offer her comfort, any way he could.

He had no clue how long the two of them stood there, she trembling with emotion, anxiety, he holding her…wanting her. Soon, though, her tears subsided. She pulled back then. Studied his face in silence…

And something happened. Something phenomenal. No, *something magical.*

The night—the moment—turned incredibly surreal.

*Un*real.

The color of her eyes intrigued him. A blue somewhere between cobalt and indigo. Her neck was willowy and pale, and he yearned to bend his head to rain kisses along the full length of it. He wanted to peel the blouse from her body. Slip her trousers down over her hips and thighs. Expose what he could only imagine would be the glorious sight of her nakedness draped in nothing but her long, flaxen hair.

Heat writhed and twisted low in his belly. A heat, a yearning that refused to be snuffed out with prudent and logical thought. If he didn't get away from this woman—now—there would be no telling…

Moonlight glowed in the incandescent mist and her eyes took on an unmistakable sultry glint. It was then that he deciphered the hunger emanating from her. Felt her passion pulsing like a thundering heartbeat. Her skin was hot to the touch. She wanted him just as much as he wanted her. So he did the only conceivable thing that came to mind.

Her lips were sweet and moist when his mouth slanted down over hers. He inhaled the luscious scent of her. The sheer tenderness of the kiss made him utter the moan just as it gathered at the back of his throat. His tongue danced and skittered across her lips, and she opened her mouth just enough so that she could take his bottom lip between her teeth. She groaned as if loving the taste of him. He felt her nipples bud to life through the thin fabric of her blouse. The wantonness of her, the lushness of her abandon, made his eyes go wide. And it was his sharp intake of breath that seemed to break the spell that had so completely ensnared them.

She drew away from him, her hands planted on his shoulders, fingertips digging into his muscles as she blinked with both alarm and fear. Clearly she was wondering just how she came to be in the arms of a stranger.

The woman pushed herself from him.

"Wait." However, his plea didn't keep her from taking a small backward step. His hands fell to his sides, his whole body feeling chilled, deprived, without the warmth of her nearness.

Almost as if they had a mind of their own, her fingers rose and pressed themselves against her still-moist lips. Again she blinked, this time in obvious shock as the realization of the moment set in.

"Listen...it's okay." Conner felt helpless. How could he possibly make sense for her of what had just happened between them when he couldn't make sense of it for himself?

Her throat convulsed in a swallow as she averted

her gaze. Then she darted one more quick glance at him before turning away.

"Don't go!" he called.

But she ran, and in a heartbeat was consumed by the trees and the thick lake mist.

Chapter One

Mattie Russell cradled the steamy cup of tea between her hands, her shock and disbelief over her conduct just as overwhelming—just as garishly vivid—in the illumination of morning as it had been when she'd raced away from the oh-so-handsome Native American who had happened upon her last night.

What in the world had compelled her to accept such intimate comfort from a stranger? And what had she been thinking when she'd surrendered to the compulsion to *kiss* him?

She'd been in too much distress to think. *That* had been the problem.

Her work was gratifying. But she was often left feeling alone and vulnerable. The sacrifice. The secrecy. It got the better of her at times, just as it had last night.

Mattie sipped her tea. Yes, that had been the problem, all right.

Well…that and the fact that the man had been so darned gorgeous. Like a prince who had stepped out of some dark and mysterious fantasyland. A night prince.

The memory of his kiss, along with the heat that had churned inside her at the sound of his voice, made her shiver, even now. The magnetism she'd felt had been as unmistakable and overpowering as the pull of the tides on the seas.

Who was he? And what was he doing on what should have been a deserted corner of Smoke Valley Reservation?

Oh, she'd seen glimpses of him before last night. She was sure it was the same man. She'd even spoken to the sheriff of the Kolheek reservation, Nathan Thunder, reporting the man's presence. Nathan had said he'd look into the matter and had assured her she had nothing to fear. She'd tried to put the stranger out of her mind. And doing so hadn't been too difficult, as she'd had some real troubles to deal with over the past couple of weeks when a "special visitor" had shown up at her door. But that problem was solved, everyone safe and settled. And Mattie had found herself staring out her window, wondering about him again. Looking for him. The elusive stranger.

The small acre of ground encompassing her bed-and-breakfast butted up against reservation land. She was a short walk away from Smoke Lake, and, oh, how she loved that calm body of water. The fact that it remained unchanged, a constant that helped to root her, make her feel grounded, was a comfort.

She and her sister, Susan, had spent their youth swimming in the lake during the summer and skating on its frozen surface in the winter. Rarely had the two girls seen any of the Native Americans living there, since the main area of the reservation was on the far side of the sprawling lake.

Mattie knew there was a hunting cabin nearby, though. She'd been about nine or so the first time she and Susan had happened upon it on one of their explorations. There hadn't been much to the tiny log building, but even so, the girls hadn't dared to venture inside. Their father would have grounded them both for a week had he known they were on the reservation, let alone trespassing in someone's cabin.

Could her native prince be staying in the cabin? she wondered. But why would he isolate himself from the other Kolheeks living on the reservation? The Indians were a close-knit people who thrived on their strong sense of community and togetherness. But it seemed the stranger—her prince—was a loner.

Again Mattie's curiosity was stirred as she pondered who he was. Before she realized it, she was walking out the door, across her backyard and into the thick woods.

Mattie believed this mountainous lake area was the most beautiful, most serene place on earth. The tranquillity of the majestic elms and oaks and sugar maples called her name. And the blue-green water of Smoke Lake seemed to breathe with a life all its own. She hadn't managed to stay away from the place as a child, when her father had forbidden her to go onto the reservation, and she couldn't stay away as an adult.

She had little self-control when it came to walking these forest paths. The land belonged to the Kolheek, and she really should respect that. She sighed, but she continued to chase the echoing call of the shady woodland.

As profound and romantic as that sounded, it wasn't any esoteric call she was heeding at the moment. No, she was simply surrendering to the interest in uncovering the identity of her night prince. The man with the kiss that could melt a woman's heart.

Like a bee to a vibrantly hued, fragrant flower, she felt drawn back to the lake bank, back to the place where she'd last seen him.

Birds twittered in the treetops and small creatures scurried in the underbrush as she made her way through the forest. Narrow fingers of sunlight shafted through the leaves, turning the still air a luminous and glorious gold. She heard the cascading water of one of the small springs that fed Smoke Lake, and she smiled. There was something about all that water that calmed her soul.

She followed the snarl of berry bushes along the bank of the lake. Years of following the spongy, pine-needled lake bank told her the thorny brambles would soon part and she'd be rewarded with a fabulous view.

As always, a sigh slipped from her lips when the picture-perfect lake came into view. The dazzling fall foliage framed the water beautifully. Before she'd even exhaled completely, unexpected movement had her darting back behind the thicket. There, not a hundred yards offshore, a man swam. And although she couldn't see his face, she knew it was her prince.

Sunlight glinted off his sculpted back. His arms pumped, up and over, up and over, sending droplets flying in a straight line ahead of him as he slid effortlessly through the water.

Heavens, but he must be chilled to the bone. Yes, the air temperature was warm for October in New England, verging on an honest-to-goodness Indian summer, but the lake water must be quite raw after weeks of cool autumn days and even cooler nights.

However, her concern slipped away like sand through a loose fist, her heartbeat tripping in her chest. He certainly was a sight to behold. She watched him move farther away from her, and she realized she was smiling. Grinning, really. Her shoulders relaxed and she felt her insides go all soft and sensual.

Soft and sensual? Get real, Mattie.

She ought to be ashamed of herself. This wasn't like her at all. She was engaged in a blatant act of voyeurism. Her behavior was nothing short of wicked.

Wasn't it just too fun? Her grin widened. Finally she surrendered to the silent laughter that bubbled up from deep in her throat. She pressed her fingers to her lips to contain her humor.

And just as the pads of her fingertips met her mouth, she was reminded of the searing kiss she'd shared with the stranger. Her blood pulsed through her veins at an alarming speed.

"Steady, Mattie," she murmured quietly. "Steady."

She stifled the urge to giggle.

Lord, what on earth had gotten into her?

Far up the bank, the man's feet evidently touched the lake bottom, and he waded toward shore. His shoulders looked powerful as his back muscles bunched, his arms swinging, with each labored step through the water. He had the body of a true athlete.

His coppery skin glittered as rivulets sluiced off his body, water droplets clinging in an array of sun-glinting beads. His hair had turned to a black river down the middle of his back. Then Mattie's eyes widened, her mouth forming a tight, shocked circle when she realized he was—

Stark naked!

Her knees went weak at the sight of the cute dimples located low on his back...just above his—

Turn away, a silent voice scolded her. *Turn your head. Walk away. Give the man some privacy.*

A long list of chores awaited her at home. Keeping a bed-and-breakfast going took long hours, hard work. She should go, get started on all those household tasks needing to be done.

Still, she stared.

She couldn't take her eyes off his tight gluteus muscles. There wasn't an ounce of fat on him, and his rear was as gloriously bronzed as the rest of his body.

Then the most deliciously evil thought ran through her mind: the man's form ought to be on display in some museum...where appreciative viewers could smooth their fingertips over his taut thighs, his rippled abs, his defined...

Again she found herself grinning. Without

thought, she shifted her weight—and then went completely still, heart hammering, when she saw his head lift to attention, his gaze scanning the bank. Could he have heard her? Or did he simply sense an intruder?

She was grateful for the thick tangle of leafy bushes that provided a handy shelter. And she relaxed a bit when she saw him dive back into the lake.

This was total lunacy. She knew it just as surely as she knew her own name.

"Mattie Russell," she whispered sternly under her breath, "you should not be standing here. You should be ashamed of yourself. Completely ashamed, and I mean it."

However, the reprimand only had her pulling down a branch for a better view. She knew without a doubt that she was harboring lust in her heart, plain and simple. She was lusting after the sight of her luscious prince.

You're despicable, you know that, she silently fumed at herself. *You're nothing more than a Peeping Tom. It's atrocious.*

"It's not all that bad."

It's against the law, the silent voice warned.

"No, it isn't," she murmured right back. "He's swimming nude right out in public. Right out where everyone can see."

Everyone? the voice asked. *He's on Kolheek property. You are* not *supposed to be here.*

Mattie pressed her lips together. Her conscience was right. She was trespassing.

But did she close her eyes? Did she turn around and go home? No, she did not. What she did was mutter, "Shut up, you, and let a girl have a little fun."

Just then sunlight glinted golden on his wide, powerful back and he kicked up his feet, disappearing beneath the surface of the water.

Mattie waited—forever, it seemed to her. Mild alarm crept over her. No human could hold his breath this long, she thought. He could be caught on a sunken branch. He could have struck his head, be lying unconscious on the sandy bottom. She waited a little longer, about the span of ten thundering, panicky heartbeats. Then she moved from behind the berry brambles and inched her way closer to the bank.

Water lapped at the toes of her canvas sneakers. Her gaze searched the smooth surface of the lake, but she didn't see a single ripple. A wave of panic welled, and she wondered if she should wade out into the lake or run home and telephone for help.

A subtle masculine cough sounded behind her, and she whirled around.

His eyes were as black as pure onyx, just as she remembered, and her breath snagged in her throat.

Startled by his sudden appearance, she was bombarded by several feelings at once. Her stomach jumped with giddy nervousness. She was relieved beyond belief to realize that he was okay...that none of the frightening thoughts that had run through her mind had come to fruition as she'd stared out over the water anxiously watching for him to surface.

Hot hunger pulsed through her veins as her eyes raked down the length of his wet body.... In the back of her mind she was grateful as well as disappointed that a pair of damp, low-slung shorts covered his manly bits.

Yes, her thoughts really were in utter chaos.

Oh, Lord, she was mortified that he'd caught her voyeuristic behavior. Peeping at him through the bushes like a common...

Hey. Wait just a second. Maybe he didn't know she'd been watching him. Maybe he simply...

Fat chance, she instantly realized. The humorous, all-knowing glint suddenly flashing in his midnight eyes told her she'd been found out. Caught red-handed. The best way to save face, she decided on a whim, was to go on the offensive.

"You scared the life out of me," she accused, plunking her fists on her hips. "I thought you were done for out there when you didn't come up for air."

His dark brows rose, and a quick bolt of pleasure shot through her when she realized she'd taken him off guard. But then one corner of his sexy mouth quirked up and she knew he'd regrouped.

"As you can see..."

He wasn't working very hard to cover the amusement in his tone.

"The, ah, source of your entertainment—"

His eyes took on a teasing glint and the flirtation in his gaze made her toes curl.

"—is just fine."

Yes, he is mighty fine, a naughty voice in her head commented.

Mattie had to tuck her top lip between her teeth to keep from grinning. She should be ashamed. Dreadfully so. But for some reason, she wasn't. Instead, there seemed to be a playful child in her just bursting at the seams to get out.

"Yes," she murmured, "I can see that."

Obviously recognizing the compliment just as she intended it, he smiled then, and it seemed as if she was feeling the full heat of the sun for the first time in her whole life. He had a wonderful smile. A gorgeous smile. A smile that made a woman's thoughts go completely blank.

After a moment she forced herself to admit, "I guess I owe you an apology. But you know, you really shouldn't be swimming, um, all natural like out here where everyone can see."

His brows rose again. "Everyone?"

"Well, okay." She yielded the point, not failing to note that his observation mirrored her very own argument with her conscience just a few minutes before. She amended, "Where *I* can see, then."

Lifting his golden chin, he laughed. The sound of it made her go all shivery. She laughed, too.

"Point taken," he finally said.

"Mattie Russell." She offered him her hand.

His palm slid into hers, and she was walloped with a quavering swelter.

"I own a B and B not too far away." She hoped the turmoil taking place inside her wasn't evident in her voice.

"Freedom Trail?"

The surprise that shot through her showed on her face, she was sure. "You've heard of my place?"

"I grew up on the rez. The B and B has been in operation for years, hasn't it?"

She nodded. "Freedom Trail has always been my

home. My parents met when my mom was in her late thirties, and my dad was in his early forties. They married and bought the B and B. My sister and I were both born there.'' She smiled. ''We had a ball growing up around here.''

''Your parents still running the place?''

''No,'' she told him. ''They've retired to Florida.'' She shoved away the painful thoughts of the funeral that had so drastically changed all of their lives.

''So,'' he said, ''you now run the place with your sister?''

It was an innocent guess on his part. Mattie's lips pressed into a thin line, and she took a deep breath. ''No. My sister died five years ago.''

''I'm sorry.''

Sympathy turned his eyes a soft sable. Mattie feared he'd ask questions about Susan…questions she wasn't quite strong enough to answer without feeling guilty and getting teary eyed and upset. The best thing to do, she decided, was to quickly change the subject.

''So, um,'' she hedged, ''what should I call you?''

Other than my night prince, the mischievous voice in her head added.

He looked contrite. ''I'm sorry. I'm Conner Thunder.''

She knew of the Thunder family. They were prominent members of Smoke Valley Reservation, and she knew his cousins Grey and Nathan and grandfather Joseph. But his name sounded more familiar to her than it should, and she couldn't put her finger on why exactly.

Then, like a bolt of lightning from the blue, it

came to her. Conner Thunder's name had been mentioned in the local newspaper when the Kolheek Community Center was being planned. He and his contracting company had received some bad press locally when he'd refused to come from Boston to the reservation to help build the center. Then several months ago she'd read about him again, something about a tragic accident that had happened on one of his job sites. An accident that had landed him in court. The journalist had actually had the audacity to suggest that fate had somehow paid Conner back for his repudiation. The whole business, with its one-sided commentary, had left a bad taste in her mouth.

Mattie remembered thinking what a shame it was for the reporter to write such a vicious thing about someone else. Someone who was unable to defend himself. Still, she'd also remembered wondering why a member of the Kolheek tribe—a strongly cohesive community—would refuse to help his people.

Although she smiled at Conner Thunder, she suspected the thoughts running through her head had caused a crease to form on her brow.

Conner fancied himself a people person. In his line of work, interacting with all kinds of people day in and day out, he had to be. He was good at sensing the ever-changing human disposition. He could read faces, decipher body language, and he had watched Mattie Russell run the gamut of emotions this morning.

He'd been delighted to see her smooth porcelain skin tinge pink with embarrassment when he'd slipped up behind her. She'd made a meager attempt at defensiveness, but those blue eyes had sparkled with a flirtation that had his whole body thrumming with awareness. She certainly was a vivacious woman. She'd quickly relaxed enough to tell him a little about her family and Freedom Trail. But right now, he sensed, she was disturbed about something.

His interest in her had been sparked when he'd come upon her last night at the lake. Her sobs had almost broken his heart. The urge to ask what had upset her to such a degree had been nearly overwhelming. But he'd curtailed it. When he'd reached for her, he'd meant only to offer her comfort, offer her a strong shoulder to cry on. The Great One above knew she surely needed it. But something had ripped logic clean out of his head and he'd ended up kissing her.

The kiss they had shared had rocked him to the marrow. She'd filled his thoughts for hours last night. Even his dreams had been invaded by her. And that had turned out to be both a blessing and a curse. Her invasion into his head—into his dreams—had overpowered the vague and haunting nightmare that had been plaguing him lately. But even though the wholly carnal dreams of her had replaced his frightening vision, he'd still ended up waking with his heart pounding, his mind pleading for answers, his tense body experiencing a different kind of ache altogether.

Some of the niggling questions he'd had about her were answered now, like her name, where she lived. He also realized that the darkness and the lake mist hadn't been playing tricks on his eyes when they'd first met. She was just as gorgeous as he'd remembered. She was petite, willowy, with soft, generous curves in all the right places.

While offering her comfort, he really shouldn't have noticed the firmness of her breasts pressed against his chest, or the narrowness of her waist, or the luscious curve of her hip. But he had.

"I haven't seen you around town," she commented.

Again he got the distinct impression that she was preoccupied with something. Ever since he'd revealed his name, the easy air between them had become tense. Curious, he thought.

"I've been away from home for a while," he told her. His eyes skipped over the trees and the crystalline water. "And I never realized how much I'd been missing Smoke Lake and the rez."

The reservation was located near the town of Mountview on the southwestern edge of Vermont's Green Mountain National Forest. He enjoyed this lush environment, and now that he thought about it, he really had no idea what had kept him away so long.

"I haven't been back for years, in fact."

Something about that confession was disquieting for him.

Mattie lifted a hand and tucked a strand of her long blond hair behind her ear. She cocked her head a fraction, her gaze glittering, and he thought some mischievous forest sprite had knocked the breath clean out of his chest.

She said, "Then I'll bet your grandfather was happy to see you."

My, he thought. With that smile, Mattie Russell could charm the blue right out of the sky.

"You know my grandfather?" he asked.

Mattie's head bobbed. "I've…met him."

Conner felt compelled to admit, "I haven't seen him yet."

Surprise was evident in her delicate features. "Well, why on earth not?"

"As far as I know, he doesn't even know I'm here."

Bewilderment clouded her pretty blue gaze. "I don't understand."

He took a slow, deep inhalation, hoping to give himself time to formulate his words…time to decide how much to tell.

"To be frank, I'm…well, I'm avoiding people these days," he began, the hesitation in his voice evident even to him. "While I work out a few things." He moistened his lips. "This is a great place to reflect and think."

Her·expression told him she understood the serenity offered by the New England mountains. But he could see his obscure response stirred her curiosity. He steeled himself for her to probe further.

She surprised him by softly commenting, "It's good to reflect and think and work things out."

Relief swept through him. Evidently she sensed his reluctance to talk about his problems and was letting him know she was okay with that. Perceptive woman.

"I can't stay away from Boston too long," he told her. "I've got a business to run." Spurred by the interest flickering in her expression, he continued,

"I'm a contractor. I love working with my hands. I started out working as a carpenter...."

Why he was giving her the lowdown on his life's achievements he had no idea. Mattie Russell just seemed to invite him to do so.

"Constructing private homes, mostly. But I gradually moved into contracting bigger projects. Office buildings. Business complexes. Shopping malls. That kind of thing."

Her eyes lit up, as though some great idea had occurred to her, and Conner felt his blood heat up and chug through his veins. His physical reaction to her had his words slowing to a crawl.

"What?" he finally asked, unable to quell his smile any longer. "Did I say something funny?"

"Oh, no." She shook her head, and the ends of her long blond tresses whipped to and fro. "I was just thinking, is all."

He didn't bother voicing a request, just cocked his head a fraction and waited for her to expound. She didn't disappoint him.

"So...you have...skills. You know how to build things."

She didn't form the thoughts as questions. Folks rarely did. Like a doctor who is constantly barraged with medical issues from complete strangers, Conner was often hit up for free advice regarding the how-tos of carpentry. But Mattie Russell was obviously too polite to actually ask for advice without first receiving some kind of permission from him.

He smiled. "Sounds like you might have need of a carpenter."

"I do!"

Animation had her expression brightening, and he couldn't help but note how gorgeous Mattie Russell was.

"I have a carriage house on my property," she continued. "I've been wanting to renovate it, make it into a bridal suite of sorts. A honeymoon cottage. It would offer the newlyweds who stay at the inn a bit more privacy. It would be so great if you'd come take a look at the building. Tell me if it's worth renovating. Maybe give me a few expert suggestions."

Conner's first impulse was to jump at the chance— any chance—to be near the beautiful and vivacious Mattie. But logic had him putting on the brakes. He'd taken a sabbatical from his work, from his life, really, in order to solve the mystery of the dreams that continued to plague him.

But he'd been back on the rez for weeks, yet he'd received no breakthrough regarding these images, had received no great revelation. The isolation was getting to him. He was getting restless. Edgy. Hadn't it been that very frustration that had sent him prowling out into the darkness last night?

Maybe, just maybe, he'd been concentrating too deeply on his own problems. If he had something besides himself to focus on, maybe the answer he'd been looking for would come to him. All she was asking was that he come to take a look at her carriage house. How much trouble could that be? None at all, he decided.

The silence had drawn out, bringing on a stiffness that hadn't been there before. She took a backward step.

"I'm sorry." She lifted her palms in apology.

"That was terribly forward of me. You obviously came here looking for privacy. The last thing you need is for someone to take advantage—"

"Now, Mattie," he gently interrupted, liking the sound of her name on his lips. "You weren't taking advantage. You merely asked for some advice."

She looked up at him, and heat churned low in his gut.

After a moment of silence she asked, "You free Saturday evening? I don't have any guests due at Freedom Trail this weekend. You could take a quick look at the carriage house, then we could eat dinner. I'd love to fix you something special." Her smile spread into a grin. "I'd like to somehow atone for, um…"

That impish light was back, dancing in her eyes, and Conner thought it was entrancing.

"Somehow atone for my sins, so to speak."

He knew she was referring to the fact that she'd taken full advantage of the entertainment he'd offered her during his morning swim.

"Aw, now," he said. "I don't know that I'd call it a sin."

She flushed to the roots of her blond hair. "My mother sure would."

Conner chuckled, and she quickly joined him.

"So you'll come to dinner Saturday?"

His eyes searched her beautiful face. How could he say no?

Chapter Two

Mattie picked up the throw pillow from the couch and gave it a good thump. She'd fluffed the thing at least half a dozen times, she knew. Disgusted with her wrought-up state, she tossed the pillow next to the sofa's padded arm. But she immediately reached down to arrange it in a more inviting position.

Why on earth was she so nervous? She'd entertained what must be hundreds of people over the years at the inn. She could coax conversation from the shyest of individuals. She could have the most serious folks laughing and enjoying themselves in a matter of mere minutes. Entertaining was her forte. Amusing her guests, diverting them from their regular, workaday lives was what kept people coming back to her B and B. It's what had her guests urging their friends to come to stay at Freedom Trail, as well.

Feeding one man dinner shouldn't have her all atwitter like this.

But her night prince wasn't any ordinary man. No way. No how. She'd realized that from the first instant she'd set eyes on him.

Conner Thunder was a devastatingly attractive man. A man who intrigued her beyond measure. Her fascination with him had been such that she'd fallen into his arms the first night they had met. That was saying something significant, indeed.

Her sideline occupation allowed her to see the ugly underbelly of marriage and relationships...the dark side of the male of the species. Now, Mattie wasn't stupid enough to think that all men were controlling and abusive, that all men had serious issues when it came to dealing with anger, but it was inevitable that her experiences had forced her to develop a thick layer of reservation where men were concerned. Yet her night prince had somehow lulled to sleep that deep sense of hesitation. She'd kissed the man before she'd even known his name.

Oh, yes, she was desperately attracted to him. There was no doubt about that.

However, there was something about Conner's situation that seemed a little ''off'' to her. No matter how attractive she found the man, she'd be foolish not to admit that there was something that was not quite right about his homecoming. Why would a man return to the place of his childhood and keep himself isolated from his family? From his community?

There had to be a reason behind this lone-wolf behavior. And until she discovered what it was, she'd be an idiot to surrender to mere physical urgings.

The brass door knocker announced his arrival, and Mattie nearly jumped out of her skin. Despite the niggling thoughts that had plagued her only a moment before, a delicious shiver trilled down the full length of her spine and she hurried to the foyer.

The first thing she was cognizant of when she opened the door was his smile. She found the flash of his white teeth, the curl of his luscious lips to be utterly charming. He offered her a fistful of wildflowers, their petals an explosion of yellows and reds. Her heart melted.

''Why, thank you, sir.'' She accepted the bouquet and stepped back, inviting him to enter.

After a quick look around him, he commented, ''Your home is beautiful.''

Mattie's smile warmed. ''Thanks. Mom and Dad did all the decorating. The antiques they found are so perfect, I haven't felt the need to change a thing. I update the paint every couple of years, keep on top of the general wear and tear, but other than that, the house is just as it was when I was a kid. You want to look around?''

''Absolutely.''

She showed him the front parlor, a formal room used for afternoon teas and quiet conversations. The dining room boasted a fireplace made of local, hand-hewn rock and a long maple table and chairs polished to a rich patina only years of use could produce. As they went through the kitchen, Mattie took a moment to fill an antique crystal vase with water for the flowers. She set them on the small round table that she'd set for the very informal meal she had planned. Then she led him into the great room, the gathering place of the inn. Guests usually listened to music here after returning from dinner in town, they socialized with other guests or simply relaxed with a glass of wine as they enjoyed the marvelous view of the surrounding valley.

A fire flickered in the deep hearth and Mattie had candles burning on both the coffee table and the stone mantel. The wide French doors flanking the fireplace were the perfect frame for the countryside, which was spectacular in every season, but especially so in the fall.

"This house is just great," he said once again, stopping to pick up a large paperweight that sat on a table.

Mattie nodded. "Holds loads of good memories for me."

Absently he smoothed his fingers over the glass orb, and Mattie's eyes riveted on his hands, wishing his touch was roving over her skin rather than the heavy paperweight. The wholly unexpected thought had her eyes widening a fraction.

"This came from the rez." He indicated the intricate blown-glass ball as he set it back down on the tabletop. "Looks like Cory Snow-Rabbit's work."

"It is," she told him. "I do what I can to support the artisans of Smoke Valley. I don't know if you know this, but besides Cory's glass gallery, the Kolheek have several wonderful painters, a talented basket weaver…even a silversmith."

Conner glanced out the window toward the valley below. "No," he murmured, "I didn't know."

"In recent years," she continued, "people who had been born on the reservation and had moved away are now returning. The place is growing by leaps and bounds. They've built a new community center and a new elementary school.''

An obvious discomfort crept over him and immediately Mattie felt guilty. Her report on reservation happenings hadn't been completely innocent. Her intent had been to get him to reveal something about himself, about his reasons for staying away from his home for so long, something about his remaining apart from the tribe now that he had returned.

Finally he murmured, ''I had heard about the community center.''

Awkwardness slipped between them, and Mattie was well aware that it was all her fault.

''Well, now you're back,'' she offered brightly. ''You can see everything for yourself. The artists and their shops, the community center, the school. Everything.''

Their gazes connected, held.

''I'll do that.''

The timbre of his voice caressed her, but his expression remained somber. The moment grew more intense than she could bear and she was forced to let her eyes slide from his.

''Is that the building you want to renovate?'' he asked.

She nodded. ''That's the carriage house, yes.''

He moved toward one of the doors leading outside. ''Let's go have a look at it.''

Mattie followed him out onto the deck, down the steps and across the yard, acutely aware of the solid mass of him. He moved easily, with grace, like someone who was confident with both his body and its ability.

He stopped and studied the building with a critical eye. "Nice solid structure." He circled to one side, then the other. "Foundation is sound. You'll need new windows. And a new door."

Conner unlatched the wide door and let it swing open. He stepped inside and Mattie followed.

He whistled. "It's been a long time since I've seen a floor made of these wide oak planks."

"They won't have to be covered up, will they?" she asked. "I was hoping to have the floor sanded down and refinished."

"Would be a sin to do anything else."

It pleased her to see that they were thinking alike.

They talked about the placement of the bathroom that would need to be added. Conner told her to be sure to have insulation placed in the space between the rafters and the ceiling. He even suggested putting in a wood-burning stove to lend a cozy atmosphere.

"Several weeks of work," he said, "and this place could be transformed into a nice little hideaway for your newlywed guests."

Actually, Mattie hadn't been entirely honest about her intentions for the carriage house. She didn't want it as a honeymoon cottage at all, but as a place in which her "harbored" guests could feel safe, tucked out of harm's way, while they tried to get their lives back on track.

She was relieved to hear that Conner felt the project she had in mind was achievable.

Ever since they'd entered the carriage house, Mattie had sensed a low thrumming, a purr that stirred the air, as if some invisible undercurrent were swirling around the two of them. She could feel his eyes on her, and she looked into his handsome face.

His onyx gaze was too intense for words. His tone was whisper soft as he said, "Has anyone ever told you how good you smell? Like rain-washed skies. Like…flowers warmed by the sun."

He actually looked embarrassed by the words that had spewed from his mouth, and she thought his chagrin was more enticing than anything she'd ever seen in her life. She felt flattered by the compliment, yet at the same time she was overwhelmed with self-consciousness. Words failed her, and all she could do was smile a silent thank-you.

The air seemed to grow stifling, and she finally blurted, "We should go eat. I'd planned to serve dessert on the deck, and I don't want to miss the sunset."

His expression was unreadable. "Of course," he told her.

The trek across the lawn might have been made in a hush, but there was nothing quiet about the thoughts racing through Mattie's head, about the feelings surging through her body.

The spacious kitchen had always been her favorite room in the rambling house. As Conner opened and poured the wine, she broiled the brochette. The thinly sliced and marinated steak was juicy, the chunky vegetables crisp-tender as she slipped them off the skewers onto a bed of saffron-flavored rice minutes later. It was a simple and succulent meal that never failed to raise compliments from her dinner guests.

As they ate, that head-fogging allure abated

enough that their smiles were once again easy, the air between them light. They swapped childhood stories.

Conner told her, "I was raised by my grandfather Joseph."

Mattie knew the shaman, had welcomed him into her home; however, the habit of secrecy kept her from relating this information. She never talked about her side work to strangers. Never. And even though she felt attracted to Conner Thunder, he was still very much a stranger to her.

His dark gaze sparked attractively. "He taught me and my cousins to dive and swim, hunt and track. He instilled a fierce sense of competition between us." He grinned. "None of us would admit to fear or doubt while honing our skills and learning new ones. Cultivating competition among males is the age-old Kolheek way, I suppose."

Mattie shook her head. "With such a strong rivalry, it's a wonder one of you didn't get hurt."

"Grandfather always stopped us before we could do anything foolish." Conner chuckled. "Not that we didn't try." Then he sobered. "One would think that my grandfather's method of parenting us would have caused division among us, but that wasn't so. Grandfather also fostered in us a deep love for each other. We were more like brothers than cousins. We respected each other. Loved one another. When I was a kid, my cousins and I were inseparable." Again he laughed. "We could fight among ourselves like wildcats, but just let an outsider jump in and we'd gang up against the poor guy."

Curious now, Mattie commented, "It sounds as if

you actually grew up under the same roof as your cousins.''

"I did."

She was unable to contain her surprise.

"All three of Grandfather's sons died," Conner explained. "And two of his daughters-in-law. He raised five of his six grandchildren when, one by one, our parents either died or left the reservation. The five of us he raised were all boys. Joseph hasn't seen his only granddaughter in years. My aunt Holly took her from the reservation. They never came back."

"So all of Joseph's sons died before they could raise their own children," Mattie summed up softly. "How sad."

The Kolheek shaman had often counseled the women she took in. And each time Mattie met Joseph, she noticed that a deep sense of desolation seemed to emanate from him. No wonder. She realized now that he had suffered a great deal of sorrow during his lifetime.

Parents aren't supposed to outlive their children. Mattie could almost hear her own mother's voice as they had bowed their heads at Susan's grave site. It seemed that Joseph Thunder and Mattie's parents had something in common.

Burying one's child…the very idea seemed to go against the laws of nature. Yet Joseph had laid to rest not one, but three sons. And two of his sons' wives. Mattie couldn't imagine enduring such loss.

"My mother died when I was just a baby," Conner told her. "I have no memory of her at all. My father was killed by a drunk driver when I was six. Head-on collision. He never had a chance."

"Conner, I'm sorry." She reached out and placed her finger on his forearm. Touching his bronze skin was like coming into contact with a candle flame that licked, icy hot, at her fingertips. She inhaled deeply, slowly, in an attempt to stifle her intimate response. She eased her hand away. He didn't seem to notice her reaction, thank goodness.

However, the appreciation expressed in his midnight gaze made her flush with heat, made her heart trip against her ribs, and she was certain he must have noticed the blush she felt rushing upward, burning her cheeks with color. He was the most handsome man she'd ever met. She'd never responded to anyone in this purely physical way.

As she sat there pondering all he'd said regarding the loving relationships he'd shared with his grandfather and cousins, she was once again amazed by the fact that he'd stayed away from his childhood home, from his family, for so long. The reasons behind his absence intrigued her beyond measure.

"You said your parents were retired," Conner said, changing the subject.

Mattie realized it was her turn to talk. She told Conner how her mom and dad had moved to Belle Glade on Florida's famed Lake Okeechobee.

"They're doing well," she said. "They've even visited Mickey Mouse a few times." Chuckling, she told him all about the vacation she had taken with her parents to Walt Disney World a few years ago. "You should have seen me. I was just like a kid."

He murmured, "I wish I had."

There was a lull in the conversation, but the silence that settled between them wasn't uncomfortable. Conner picked up his glass by the stem and drained the last sip of wine from it.

"Your sister," he said, "died very young."

Mattie felt as if she'd swallowed a small, jagged rock rather than the bite of soft rice she'd just been chewing. A frown furrowed her brow. She took a moment to pull herself together, but quickly realized she simply couldn't venture down this path.

All she could say in answer was, "Yes, she did."

She set down her fork, then dabbed the corners of her mouth with her linen napkin and slid her chair back from the table.

"It's almost time for the sun to set," she announced, hearing the false brightness in her own tone. "We don't want to miss it. There's a bottle of dessert wine chilling in the ice bucket on the counter. You grab that and a couple of fresh glasses from the cabinet there." She pointed. "I'll get the platter of fruit and cheese, and we'll go out on the deck."

She bustled around the kitchen handing out orders in an attempt to avoid talking about Susan. Only a fool would have failed to notice her anxiety. Conner was no fool.

His fingers closed over her wrist. "I'm sorry." His face was grave. "I'd never have brought up the subject had I known it was going to upset you."

He had no idea of the magnitude of guilt she lived with every day, knowing that she'd failed to save her sister's life. Or that it was that unconquerable remorse that spurred her on, kept her isolated, working in secret to try to help women who found themselves in the same sort of circumstances Susan had been in. However, no matter how many women Mattie aided, it never seemed to ease her guilt over the one she'd failed.

His skin was warm against hers. Her gaze met his. "It's still very hard for me," she said.

Conner simply nodded, then turned to complete the tasks she'd set out for him, by reaching for the wine on the counter.

The sky was glazed with an array of glorious color ranging from a rich fuchsia to a streaky purple. Long, narrow clouds stretched out, gilded in radiant gold light. Mattie set the tray of cheese, grapes, apple slices and orange sections on the glass-topped patio table. Conner stood transfixed as he surveyed the wonder before him.

She moved beside him, slipping a juicy grape into her mouth before resting her forearms on the wide deck railing.

"Glorious view, don't you think?"

He nodded silently. There was awe in his regal profile. In fact, his features held an intensity that could easily have been called reverent. Worshipful. And Mattie prickled with sudden self-consciousness as if she were intruding on a very private moment.

Softly he said, "I'm sure this is what brings your visitors back again and again. It is—" he dragged his gaze from the horizon, and in the instant it took him to search Mattie's face, she felt as if she could drown in the depths of his deep, intensely black gaze "—nearly as beautiful as you."

The air grew dense and it seemed to hitch in the back of her throat when she attempted to inhale. She couldn't speak, couldn't think.

He handed her a glass. She took it from him, her

movements that of an automaton—sluggish, mech-anical.

"Of course," he continued smoothly as he poured wine, first for her, then for himself, "it could also be your awesome cooking that brings people back here. Dinner was delicious."

Her lips curled. Oh, my. What she needed more than anything was to put a little space between them. Give herself time to regroup, time to think and gather together her wits that seemed scattered all about her feet. It was as if the man had pulled the rug right out from under the soles of her shoes and she was rolling and tumbling through space.

He set the bottle on the deck railing and lifted his glass.

"To new friends," he toasted.

The wine tasted sweet and fruity on her tongue. She was subconsciously aware of many things—the smooth crystal stem between her fingers, the fresh autumn breeze, the vibrant cast of the heavens over-head. But she was so swept away by the man stand-ing next to her that it was impossible to hold on to a single thought for longer than a second or two be-fore it went skittering off just out of reach.

"Mattie…"

Whatever else Conner had been about to say ebbed into oblivion as he, too, seemed to become tangled up in…in…well, in whatever it was that had carried her off and stolen away all thought. He was going to kiss her again. Oh, she'd dreamed of this moment since their lips had first touched.

His fingertips scorched their way along the sensi-tive underside of her jaw. His wine-sweet breath brushed her skin as he drew ever closer. And then his mouth covered hers.

Hot. Luscious.

The heated male fragrance that was his alone filled her nostrils, and she closed her eyes to better savor the scent of him, the taste of him. Blindly she reached up with her free hand and combed her fingers through his long hair.

His tongue danced across her lips, enticing, tempting…persuading her to grant him entrance into the secret recesses of her mouth. With no hesitation she parted her lips, and he deepened the kiss.

Mattie felt as if she were swooning. That if she didn't hold on to Conner firmly, she'd lose her balance and plunge head over feet into the passion igniting her soul.

He was feverish with desire, too. She sensed it in the urgency of his touch. Tasted it in his kiss. Felt it in the electric hum that fairly pulsed from him.

His breathing was rushed, and his heart pounded against his ribs…against the palm she'd splayed on his hard chest.

Realizing that he was as totally enmeshed as she by the wanton energy throbbing between them seemed only to heighten her own desire. Sliding her fingers along the sharp angle of his jaw, she drew him nearer, ever nearer, with her eyes, with her touch, with her *need*.

Mattie heard a groan, and didn't know if it had been murmured by herself or Conner. But did it matter, really? She didn't want to think. Didn't want to try to figure out anything. All she wanted was to become lost in the moment.

She felt her body grow more pliant. Her joints loosened, her muscles relaxed. There was no resistance in her. But then he unrepentantly slid his hand over her breast, and her nipples hardened to nubs. She was so startled by the heat of his touch, by her body's reflexive reaction, that she couldn't stop the gasp that rushed from her throat.

Immediately he drew back, the passionate craze that had held him spellbound and hazed his crow-black eyes fading like a waning tide. Taking its place was an obvious sense of confusion...and a hefty dose of contrition.

"I'm sorry, Mattie." He stepped away from her, absently brushing back the length of blue-black hair that had fallen over his shoulder. "I should never have let that happen."

Disappointment welled up in her, smacking her square in the face and stilling the fierce thudding of her heart. That he saw the kiss as a mistake upset her greatly.

"I haven't been sleeping well," he continued. "I'm sure exhaustion has my mind fogged. Adding to that the wine...the atmosphere—" He looked out at the magnificent twilit sky, one shoulder shrugging, and when he looked at her again, apology was thick in his gaze. "I guess I just got carried away."

Carried away. Mattie thought that was a pretty good description of what had just taken place between them. However, she had no intention of apologizing for her participation in the awesome moments the two of them had just shared.

Reaching for his wineglass, she slipped it from his grasp. "Maybe I should make us some coffee."

She tried not to feel hurt by the fact that he insisted on offering excuses for his behavior.

"And it's getting chilly out here," she said. "We should go inside."

She gathered up the dessert tray that they hadn't even touched and motioned for Conner to follow her into the house.

"Have a seat," she told him. "Relax. I'll be right back with some coffee."

Mattie made short work of filling the coffeemaker with ground beans and water, and as the coffee brewed, she stood with her hip resting against the counter, her fingers worrying her chin.

Never in her life had another human being filled her with such delight, such longing, such excitement. Since meeting Conner Thunder merely days ago, Mattie felt as if her whole life had brightened.

Yes, she'd already realized that he'd somehow short-circuited her usual hesitance and constraint where men were concerned. Why, she couldn't help but wonder, should she feel cautious about a man who had done nothing but give to her? He'd been so generous and comforting the night they had first met. And he hadn't even known her name then. She'd been a complete stranger to him, yet he'd held her, let her lean on him, offered her a solace she had never before experienced. That had to account for something.

Disappointment had walloped her when he'd expressed regret over the kiss they'd shared out on the deck just now. The fact that she didn't want him feeling sorry that he'd kissed her was a sure sign of...of—

Well, she didn't care to look too closely at her own emotions right now.

What was amazing to her was his willingness to take the brunt of the blame for the passionate incident. That meant something significant. The men she was used to dealing with in her work with the abused were nearly always censuring and critical, tending more often to point the finger of fault than take responsibility for anything that was happening in their lives. She'd played just as strong a role as he had in those sensuous moments out under the sunset, yet he'd held himself totally accountable. That spoke volumes for his character, didn't it?

Mattie decided that it did.

She also decided, chuckling softly to herself, that she was doing all she could to play up Conner's finer points just so she wouldn't have to feel remorseful for desiring him.

The rich aroma of coffee wafted around her, urging her to turn to the cupboards for cups, saucers and spoons. She poured the coffee and placed the steaming cups on a tray, then reached for the sugar bowl and cream pitcher.

Excitement twittered in her belly as she picked up the tray. She suddenly felt a giddy determination to explore why he felt the need to apologize for what had happened between them out on the deck. Surely he could tell that she'd wanted him to kiss her. Surely he'd understood the feelings and heated need that he incited in her.

She entered the living room, and the anticipation in her chest subsided, her shoulders rounding softly when she saw that he'd fallen asleep. Quietly placing the tray on a side table, she spooned sugar into one cup of coffee and stirred.

She sat in the chair adjacent to the couch.

A gorgeous man is asleep on your sofa. A silent voice spoke from somewhere in the back of her brain. Her smile broadened of its own accord.

She sipped at her coffee, letting her eyes travel down the length of him. He was tall and broad. His long, tapered fingers were laced together at his waist. His trousers covered a flat stomach, narrow hips, muscular thighs.

A heady contentment settled over Mattie. Owning a B and B, she knew that people often had a difficult time falling asleep in a new place. Did this mean Conner was comfortable here? With her?

Whoa there, girl, her brain warned. Don't go making too much of this. Hadn't he said he'd been having trouble sleeping? That he was suffering from exhaustion?

Still, Mattie had to admit that she liked the idea of having Conner around. Sleeping on her couch. Better yet, sleeping in her bed. Better still, *not* sleeping in her bed. Her mouth pulled back into a languorous grin as she conjured up all sorts of deliciously sinful images of her and Conner tangled in cool cotton sheets.

Wow! Now, wouldn't *that* cure her loneliness?

However, her smile faded dead away as she thought of the reason behind the seclusion she was forced to suffer. Keeping her shelter a secret was a necessary and awesome task. A task that demanded Mattie ignore her own needs and focus solely on the abused women who were desperate for her help.

Then those worrisome doubts recurred. Yes, it was fun to toy with the idea of romantic kisses and longing gazes, but it would be remiss of her not to take the hard facts into full account.

She didn't know this man. She might feel attracted to him, she might have eaten dinner with him, she might even have shared some childhood stories with him. But he was a stranger, nonetheless. And there was something odd about how he was keeping himself secluded in the woods of the reservation. That seed of skepticism had already been planted in the fertile soil of her mind, hadn't it? She could not turn a blind eye to such curious behavior.

Until she knew more about him, until she discovered the reason behind his peculiar living arrangements, she didn't dare trust him with the knowledge that she harbored women who were on the run.

It had taken Mattie years to assemble the small group of trusted friends and professionals who aided these women who had been let down by law enforcement, by the courts, by the health-care system… women who had tried every other means to have happy lives, but had failed.

Mattie had gone to visit Joseph Thunder many, many times, trying to get a handle on whether or not he could be trusted to help her. In the end, the noble shaman had proved to have the deep sense of honor and dependability that was so well-known of the Kolheek tribe of Native Americans. And after many talks with Mattie, Dr. Grey Thunder had proved himself to be trustworthy, as well.

A tiny knot formed in her stomach as she watched Conner sleep. He'd admitted that he hadn't been to visit his grandfather—that he hadn't even let the man know he'd returned to the reservation. That piece of the puzzle confused Mattie. It suggested that all was not right between Conner and his family. Her brow puckered as her desire to alleviate her loneliness warred with the gut feeling that she really should practice a little common sense. If not for herself— which should have been reason enough—then for the women she sheltered.

She set the coffee cup on the table by the chair, the taste of the coffee having gone suddenly flat.

Conner had told her that he'd left Smoke Valley years ago and hadn't returned. Had he also turned his back on the honorable life of the Kolheek?

Suspicion mounted, leaving her feeling ashamed that she'd been all too willing just moments ago to shove aside every uncertainty regarding Conner for a few moments of bliss in his arms.

Sure, there might be simple and completely plausible answers to all her questions about the man who slept on her couch. However, Mattie was forced to come to one definite conclusion: until she knew for certain that Conner was worthy of her trust, she must fight the strong attraction she felt for him. Placing her faith in a stranger could be dangerous for the women she took in. For the future of her work. *For herself.*

Again she thought of the vulnerability of the battered women who were desperate for help, and Mattie decided then and there that she'd rather spend her life alone and lonely rather than hurt even one of them.

No sooner had she come to this sad conclusion than Conner emitted a soul-haunting moan that made her heart leap to her throat.

Chapter Three

Why couldn't he make out the booming voices? Why couldn't he focus in on the hulking forms moving before him? The haze was too thick for him to be certain of anything. The very air seemed to have turned viscous...a glutinous gunk that muffled sound, blurred vision. And the heat. Scorching. More than he could possibly bear.

But was the heat emanating off the massive angry forms? Or was it radiating from the place itself? Had he descended into the very bowels of Mother Earth, where rock melted into rivers of lava?

Fear oozed from his pores. He felt small. Helpless. Cowering against the heat. Against the anger. Against the terror.

Something horrifying was about to happen. Something he couldn't stop.

His skin crawled and instinct had him flinching...cringing into an even smaller ball when icy claws grabbed at his arm. Conner's eyes opened wide and he inhaled sharply, his heart thudding.

The dream. He'd gotten sucked into it again.

When his eyes finally focused, he saw that the claws were not claws at all, but fingers…gentle fingers on his forearm as Mattie had reached out to wake him. He must have called out or murmured or thrashed about. There was deep concern in her gemblue eyes.

"Are you okay?"

The distress in her tone warmed him right down to the soles of his feet.

"I'm fine," he told her. "I haven't had that dream since—"

Conner stopped short. He'd nearly revealed that he hadn't been plagued by the nightmare since the night he'd met her…since the night he'd first kissed her…since the night he'd begun being tormented by agonizingly sweet dreams…*of her.*

He inhaled deeply, giving himself time to shake off the fuzziness of sleep. Time to clear his mind of the bone-numbing fear that the hazy nightmare never failed to elicit. Conner straightened himself on the couch.

"I'm fine," he repeated, dry-washing his face with both hands. "Just fine. Now that I'm awake."

The couch cushion depressed as Mattie eased herself down beside him.

"You want to talk about it?" she offered. "The nightmare, I mean."

He tried to shrug it off. "It's the accident, I'm sure. The stress of it triggered a recurrence of the bad dreams I had as a child, years and years ago."

Mattie's brow knitted and she said, "I did read in the paper some time ago that there had been some kind of a problem on one of your work sites. That a worker had gotten hurt."

"Paralyzed," he corrected. "One of my men got his legs crushed beneath a forklift." His body was tense. "Toby was young, foolish. He'd come back from lunch one Friday afternoon with liquor on his breath. I gave him hell right in front of everyone. Told him to go home and sleep it off. But he didn't listen to me. In fact, he defied my orders. The minute my back was turned, he went right on working. He misjudged the space behind the forklift he was driving and rolled the whole contraption over an embankment."

Commiseration filled Mattie's expression.

"He sued, of course," he continued. "My company was cleared of any wrongdoing, but—" he shook his head "—it was an awful ordeal."

"I can imagine."

He leaned forward, resting his elbows on his knees. "The strain of it prompted these dreams to return. I've been suffering with them for months."

Funny, he hadn't been able to confide in anyone regarding the devastating anxiety he'd faced while he'd been in that courtroom, the all-consuming guilt over knowing a man he'd hired would spend the rest of his life in a wheelchair, yet here he was confessing his soul to Mattie.

"You said you had the dreams as a child." She shifted her weight on the cushion, her knee only a hairbreadth from his. "If you don't mind my asking, what happens in the dream?"

He sighed, anxiety making his shoulder muscles rock-hard. "The funny thing is, I can't really see what's happening. There's a fog, or a…cloak of some kind that's blurring my sight. But I can sense that there are two big—" he paused, groping for descriptive words "—shapes. One of them is very animated. Furious. Looming. A huge, angry bear, maybe. The other form is just as angry, but unmoving." No, he thought. That wasn't quite right. "Immovable. Like a giant oak. So much bigger than me. More frightening than hell itself."

Confusion made him frown. "But why should I fear an oak tree? It makes no sense. All I know is that I have this sense that something terrible is about to happen. Something that will change my life forever. And I want to scream. I want to make the muddled shapes stop fighting. But I'm totally paralyzed." He let his gaze settle on hers. "With fear."

Compassion deepened the color of her eyes to a clear sapphire. "Did you ever talk about this with anyone?"

"No." One corner of his mouth pulled back into a humorless grin. "Like I said, I was just a kid. In my mind, telling someone would have been made me look—" he shrugged "—weak. I couldn't reveal what was surely a vulnerability. My cousins would have had a ball calling me a sissy. No, I couldn't tell anyone about it."

That's exactly how he'd felt as a kid.

"Anyway," he continued, "the nightmare went away. I don't remember when. It just faded away. It didn't bother me again…"

"Until the accident," Mattie slowly finished for him.

He gave a small nod.

"I was certain," he said, "that once the trial was over that the stress I was feeling would be relieved and the nightmare would go away. But that hasn't happened." He paused a moment. "That's why I came home to the rez. To rest up. To find…some peace."

Some answers, really, but explaining the Kolheek belief that dreams were messages from the subconscious—from the soul—wasn't something Conner was prepared to do right now.

He looked into Mattie Russell's beautiful face, her compassionate gaze. He swallowed. Yes, just a moment before he'd felt it quite harmless to confide in her the secret of his persistent nightmare. But he suddenly felt uncomfortably exposed. What if she kept him talking and analyzing until his every thought, his every deed, had been laid bare?

Trepidation swamped him.

But wasn't that what he wanted? Wasn't that why he'd returned to the rez? To discover, once and for all, what was causing the nightmare?

Suddenly, though, he wasn't sure he was ready.

Of course you're ready, silent logic argued. *You've been haunting those woods for weeks looking for answers.*

Feeling totally confused, he rose from the couch in one fluid motion. "Listen, Mattie, I should get going. I've proved myself to be unfit company by falling asleep on your sofa. I apologize for that."

"It's all right," she told him.

She meant it. He could tell. He had no idea why, but she was making it easy for him to make a quick and effortless exit.

"You need to go home and get some rest." She walked him to the door and opened it for him. "But Conner…"

He turned to face her.

"If you need to talk—" her voice was soft, inviting "—you know where I am."

Hours later Mattie sat out on the deck wrapped in a thick wool sweater, marveling at how the moonlight and clouds cast shifting shadows over the thickly forested mountainside and valley.

So Conner had returned to Smoke Valley Reservation to heal from the trauma of the accident she'd read about in the newspaper, from the pressure of the court case, from his own sense of guilt about what had happened to the young man on the work site. Conner hadn't actually used the word *heal.* He'd said he came to rest up. To find peace. But emotional mending was what he needed.

Mattie had a sneaking suspicion that there was more to his return than all of that.

Those dreams. Those recurring nightmares.

He'd suffered them in silence as a child. How sad that sounded to Mattie. What had happened all those years ago to cause the fearful nightmares to beleaguer him so? The death of his mother? Yet Conner had told her his mother had died so young that he had no memory of her. His father's death, maybe? The shock a six-year-old child would suffer when dealing with the loss of a parent could easily manifest itself into nightmares.

Fear. Anger. The feeling of impending doom. Those emotions were normal reactions for a child facing a future without his beloved father.

But why the two shapes? she wondered. Shapes that seemed angry. Not with him, but with each other. Furious forms that seemed larger than life to him.

Mattie was no psychologist, that was certain, but it didn't take a Ph.D. to figure out how an accident that had paralyzed a man could rekindle a nightmare in which Conner *felt* paralyzed. She pulled her feet up into the seat of the chair, hugged her shins to her chest, rested her chin on her knees.

Were the nightmares somehow tied in to the fact that Conner had returned to Smoke Valley weeks ago without telling his grandfather? His avoiding Joseph could very well be completely innocent and unrelated to the dream, but she just didn't think so.

Mattie's mind churned. All of this was connected somehow. It had to be.

The phone rang, jarring the quiet night, and she went into the living room to answer it.

As she listened to the voice on the other end of the line, she let go of her thoughts of Conner and automatically slipped into her emotional armor: strength, dependability, calm and sound reason. She would need all these things.

Another woman in need was coming.

"I'll be ready," she promised. Then she replaced the receiver into its cradle and went about getting herself prepared.

* * *

In the wee hours of the morning she let the woman and child into her home through the back door. The boy looked to be about ten, his body dragging with fatigue. He refused to be separated from his mother, so Mattie quickly fixed a makeshift bed on the couch. He fell asleep almost instantly.

Her name was Brenda. She was missing an eye-tooth. Knocked out in a beating she took from her husband a week ago, Mattie learned. The fists that had struck her tonight had blackened both her eyes, broken her nose, cut a deep gash in her temple and sent her running for her life.

"He gonna kill me. He gonna kill me for sure."

The woman quaked with a bone-shattering fear that Mattie had seen before. In other women just like Brenda.

"He's not going to kill anyone," Mattie asserted firmly. "You did the right thing. You got out of a bad situation. You got your son out. I'm going to help you. Don't worry."

Her eyes were glazed over with terror that went soul deep. "I took Scotty. If he finds me, he'll kill me."

"He," Mattie discovered, was a semipro boxer who went by the name Tommie Boy. The man's coach and manager felt that Tommie Boy was talented enough to make it in the pro ring. However, over the past eighteen months Tommie Boy had lost every pro match that had been scheduled for him. It was only natural, Brenda told Mattie, for her Tommie to be frustrated, wasn't it?

"I love him," Brenda whispered through tears that fell silently down her pale cheeks. "But I can't take it no more. I'm scared to death he's gonna start in on Scotty.''

Mattie felt compelled to ask, "Tommie's never hit your son?"

Brenda's guilt-ridden gaze slid from Mattie's, telling the honest truth. When the woman finally lifted her chin, her tone was desperate as she said, "But it's not a regular thing. And not nothin' like what I get." Then her shoulders sagged. "It's gettin' worse. I know Tommie don't mean it. But he's gonna end up killing me. And then who would watch over Scotty?"

Mattie suppressed the flare of anger that ignited when she heard Brenda excuse her husband's behavior with "Tommie don't mean it." Mattie knew that what Brenda felt for Tommie wasn't love. It was a kind of psychological dependence, a sickness, just as Tommie Boy's physical abuse was a sickness, as well.

She could sympathize with Brenda's dependence. The woman measured zero on the self-esteem scale. And she had little in the way of formal education. Brenda felt stuck, hopeless, vulnerable. Mattie would do everything she could to help the woman heal physically and emotionally.

But Mattie felt nothing but contempt for the woman's husband.

She listened to Brenda talk until the sun peeked over the Green Mountain range to the east. She'd heard the same story countless times before. For one reason or another, law enforcement officers, the court system, social and health care agencies could do little to protect some women. Mattie had learned over the years that abused women could be found in every socioeconomic class. Some were highly educated. Some were not. Most had no family support system to speak of. And it wasn't uncommon for these women to have grown up in abusive homes, to have survived a succession of violent relationships. Brutality was a way of life for them. It had been the only world Brenda had ever known.

Mattie's hands had balled into white-knuckled fists when Brenda had told her that one family court judge had taken her into his private chambers and encouraged her not to press charges against her husband. The judge had claimed that Tommie Boy was the town's only chance of "getting on the map," and that it would be a shame for Brenda to do anything to thwart that. This same judge had then suggested that it would be a shame for Brenda to be pronounced an unfit mother, her son taken from her home, from her care.

"So I dropped all the charges," Brenda whispered. "Tommie knocked out my tooth as soon as the coast was clear. Said I needed to be punished. I look a fright, I know. But when I finally got up enough courage to ask if I could get my mouth fixed, Tommie said I looked fine to him, that I needed a reminder not to call the police again." She winced, seeming to remember the humiliation of it all. "But I never called the police, Mattie. The neighbor always did." Fresh tears welled in her eyes. "And them dominoes would just start falling."

The soft knock on the front door had Brenda's whole body tensing with panic. "Oh, Lordy, he's come for me." She looked ready to bolt.

"It's okay," Mattie assured the woman. "It's the doctor. Remember? When I went to put the coffee on, I told you I called Dr. Thunder. It's okay. You can trust him. Besides, he won't know your full name. I'd never betray your trust, Brenda. Never."

Mattie had seen this phenomenon before. Fear and anxiety had a way of eating at the mind, filling it with holes, until holding on to information became nearly impossible. But this would pass. Time could make both the mind and body whole again. All the woman needed was time and a place to feel safe.

"You sure it ain't Tommie?"

Mattie kept her tone gentle. "Brenda, your husband has no idea where you are." She got up, purposely moving slowly and easily. "You stay right here and I'll go answer the door."

The man standing on the wide front porch had the most gorgeous green eyes imaginable. As usual, Dr. Grey Thunder had his long black hair secured in a single braid down his back. Mattie had met the man a year or so ago when he'd returned to Smoke Valley to practice medicine on the reservation. He'd been kind enough to hire Lori Young, a woman who had found herself pregnant and fleeing an ex who insisted on stalking her. Grey and Lori had married as a means of keeping Lori safe. Then fate had stepped in—bringing love along with it—and the two were now devoted to one another. Matchmaking hadn't been Mattie's motive when she'd introduced them, but it was a title she was happy to have.

"Thanks for coming." She ushered him into the foyer.

"Where is she?" he asked.

"In the living room. But we need to go slow. She's awfully scared."

Grey nodded his understanding. He set down his black bag and shrugged into a white lab coat that had been draped over his arm. It helped the panicky women to see him as a professional. "What's her name?" He fastened a button, straightened the collar.

"Brenda."

First names only. That had been their agreement from the beginning. For the women's protection, Mattie would do what she could to hide their identities.

Again he nodded. He picked up his doctor's bag. "Let's go."

The battered Brenda looked like a cornered animal when Mattie entered the room. Softly she said, "This is Dr. Grey Thunder."

Grey stopped in the doorway, keeping his distance. "Hi, Brenda."

Alarm had Brenda gasping as her gaze flew to Mattie's face. It was almost as if Mattie could hear the woman's silent fears.

He knows my name! I don't want this man near me! I don't want any man near me!

Calmly Mattie reminded her, "First names only, remember? Grey knows you only as Brenda. He won't tell anyone that you're here. He's only here to help you."

The anxiety in the woman's muddy gaze didn't diminish much. Grey didn't move. Mattie knew he wouldn't until Brenda gave some sign of granting him permission. Treating these women with the utmost respect was the first step toward granting them a sense of empowerment.

"I...I don't want anyone to see me like this." Brenda turned away.

Mattie said, "You're hurt, Brenda. You've got a gash on your head. And it looks like your nose is broken. Grey can fix you up. You don't want to go through life with a scar on your face and a crooked nose."

The woman's shoulders sagged. "What does it matter?"

"Oh, come on, now." Mattie rounded the chair. "You might not think it matters now. But you will. In time."

Grey remained on the threshold of the room, unmoving as he waited for the woman's consent.

Finally Brenda nodded once, and the doctor approached.

"I cleaned the cut," Mattie told him. "And tried to pinch it together with a dressing tape."

"That's just fine." Grey gently eased the tape off Brenda's temple. "Doesn't look too bad. I'm going to use a bit of antiseptic ointment and then apply some surgical tape. Less chance of scarring than if I were to actually stitch it."

Mattie could see Brenda growing antsy. Thankfully, Grey worked quickly.

"Now for the nose. I'm going to have to reset it." He leaned back and looked into Brenda's eyes. "This is going to hurt."

The woman's jaw clenched, her gaze relating plainly that pain was something she was used to.

Once her nose was taped, Brenda began to weep.

"I don't want nobody to see me." Her tone was pleading. "Make him go away, Mattie."

Grey immediately began gathering his things together. "I'll come back when you're feeling stronger," he told Brenda. "You need to get some rest."

Mattie left Brenda watching over her sleeping son and walked Grey to the door.

"Here's a very mild sedative for her." He slipped a small bottle into Mattie's hand. "To help her sleep. But I'm only leaving three, and I'd like you to dole them out."

"Thanks," Mattie told him, accepting the pills. "For everything."

He paused at the door, his smile sad. "I just feel so bad that this kind of stuff has to happen. You're a good woman, Mattie Russell." He sighed, forcing himself to brighten. "Lori sends her love."

Mattie reached out and placed her hand on Grey's sleeve. "How's she feeling?"

The New Year would bring a baby to the Thunder household. Mattie was so happy that her friends had found each other.

"She's well," Grey told her. "The baby's growing every day. Her belly's getting big, much to her dismay."

He chuckled, and Mattie was very aware of the love he felt for his wife.

Then a shadow flickered across the doctor's green gaze.

"Can I ask you something, Mattie?"

"Of course," she told him. "Anything."

Grey looked discomfited, as if he wasn't quite sure

how to voice his thoughts. Finally he said, "My brother told me you'd seen our cousin Conner. That you thought he might be staying at the hunting lodge."

"Yes, I did mention that to Nathan. At the craft fair."

Hesitation tinged Grey's tone as he admitted, "I don't usually like to pry into other people's business, but I'm worried about Conner. You see, he's been back on the rez for weeks, but he hasn't come into town to see any of us. I'm…concerned."

An uncomfortable awkwardness crept over Mattie. She knew Conner was keeping himself secluded. That for reasons he hadn't made her aware of—reasons he himself might not understand—he was isolating himself from his family. Yet he'd returned to Smoke Valley looking for relief. Though she hadn't figured out Conner's circumstances, she felt that it would be somehow disloyal of her to discuss the matter with Grey.

Still, Grey had been such a great help to her. He'd volunteered his time and talent to treat the women who came to her for shelter. And the worry darkening the doctor's gaze wrenched her heart.

"I was wondering," he said softly, "if you'd seen him again? If you'd seen with your own eyes that he's okay?"

It would have been cruel of her not to relieve Grey's anxiety.

"I've seen him," she acknowledged. "He's fine. In fact, he had dinner here with me last night."

The relief this information gave Grey was evident. His brow smoothed, his eyes cleared.

"That's great," he said. He actually smiled. "I'm glad to hear he's no longer living like a hermit."

Mattie patted his forearm. "He really is okay."

Memories of Conner swarmed into her mind: the intensity in his onyx gaze, the heat in his touch, the desire in his kiss. She felt her face grow warm.

"Listen," Grey said, "if you get the chance, would you urge Conner to come visit us? We'd like to see him. All of us."

"I will," she promised. "I think that would be good...for everyone."

Grey lifted his hand in farewell and went out the door.

Chapter Four

The soft knock on her bedroom door awoke Mattie with a start. During the three days that Brenda and Scotty had been staying with her, they hadn't made a peep. The two of them had barely ventured down the stairs for any longer than it took them to eat their meals.

This hermitlike behavior was relatively normal in the women who came to stay with her. The abused had a strong psychological attachment to their abusers. It took days, often a week or more, before the battered women realized that they could actually exist on their own, that they wouldn't shrivel and die living apart from their partners, that they would continue breathing…thinking…feeling. However, discovering that they could thrive on their own was something that took months of counseling.

Slipping from beneath the sheets, Mattie pulled on her jeans and tugged a V-necked sweater over her head. "Come in, Brenda," she called, her heart racing as she wondered what would have the woman seeking her out so early.

Fear fairly pulsed from the woman—Mattie could almost feel it.

"There's a man," she said. "Out back."

Mattie slipped her feet into canvas sneakers, not bothering to tie them.

"Does he look familiar?" she asked Brenda, mentally estimating how long it would take the police to arrive should she need to summon them.

The woman shook her head. "He's dallying around that building out back."

Conner.

The name whispered through Mattie's mind like a cool autumn breeze. She hadn't seen him since he'd come for dinner. That was the same night that Brenda had arrived.

"I think I know who it is," she told Brenda. "It's okay."

It was clear the woman didn't believe her.

"But what if—"

"It's okay," Mattie repeated softly. "I'll go talk to him. See what he wants."

"Can you make him go away?"

"Let me see why he's here." Mattie paused at the doorway long enough to smooth a reassuring palm over Brenda's shoulder. "Get Scotty some breakfast. I'll be right back."

"Don't tell nobody me and Scotty are here. Tommie is lookin' for us, remember?"

"I haven't forgotten," she whispered, then offered Brenda a smile.

The built-up tension in the woman kept her from returning it. ''We'll stay upstairs till he's gone.''

The pleading in Brenda's tone echoed in Mattie's head and set her heart to aching something fierce. Susan's tone had held that same imploring quality when she'd run to Mattie for help. But time and again, her sister had made the worst mistake possible. She'd forgiven her abuser, returned to the husband who'd made promise after promise that, this time, things would be different.

Susan's short life had been filled with broken promises.

The scent of coffee hit Mattie's nostrils before she even entered the kitchen. She paused long enough to pour herself some, even as she realized she didn't need any caffeine. The prospect of seeing Conner had her feeling wide awake.

Autumn crisped the air and Mattie cradled the warm mug in her hands as she tramped across the expanse of lawn to the carriage house. The door was wide open and she stepped inside. Conner was on his knees, his rock-hard thighs straining against the fabric of his worn denims as he jotted down what looked to be a measurement on a pad of paper.

''Good morning,'' she called.

He looked up and smiled a greeting, and something astonishing happened to Mattie's insides. Her stomach knotted up, and her chest felt constricted. There was just something about this man that knocked her off-kilter.

''I'd have brought you some coffee,'' she told him, ''but I didn't know how you liked it.''

The metal tape measure snapped as he reeled it

back into its housing. He left it there on the floor with the pad and pencil and straightened. "That's okay." He crossed the few feet that stood between them. "But it does smell good. I'll just have a taste of yours, if that's okay."

"W-well, sure."

He didn't exactly take the coffee from her, just wrapped his fingers around hers and lowered his mouth to the rim, tipping the mug up just enough to get a mouthful. When he raised his head, his bottom lip was moist, glistening, and Mattie helplessly speculated what his kiss might taste like were she to have the opportunity to savor the rich coffee essence of it.

She blinked. Drew in a slow, deep breath.

"So…whatcha doing?" she asked.

"I hope you don't mind. I was making a materials list for the renovation."

"B-but," she stammered, "I only asked for some free advice the other day. I didn't expect you to do any actual work."

"I know you didn't." He nodded, a thick lock of his long black hair falling across his muscular biceps. His gaze slipped from hers as he continued, "But I've been thinking about what you want done. Refinish the floor, add a wall, insulate the rafters, put in a ceiling, replace the doors and windows, put in some plumbing and bath fixtures…"

As he made the verbal list he meandered to the far corner of the carriage house where he'd been busy measuring when she'd arrived, his mind obviously focused on the job at hand.

"It would be a fairly easy and straightforward job

to coordinate,'' he told her. ''And since you don't have any paying customers at the moment...''

''Well, that's true,'' she offered quietly. It wasn't too big a lie. Brenda and Scotty weren't giving her a penny while they stayed with her. ''But—''

However, Conner didn't seem to hear her hesitation as he barreled forward. ''Now would be as good a time as any to get this renovation done.''

He'd paced back toward her, his gaze flitting here and there. Unwittingly, he shoved his fingers through his hair. ''We need an electrician to bring this wiring up to code, a plumber to install the pipes. I can have the building inspector out here for final approval in...oh, I'd say about three weeks should be plenty of time. A month at the very most.''

''I don't know....'' Now was *not* the best time for her to do anything. She was too involved with developing a trusting bond with Brenda and Scotty, counseling them, lining up resources—a place for them to live and work and go to school just as soon as they were ready to venture out into life on their own.

But then Conner's dark gaze leveled on hers, and something in his eyes made every thought of her needy guests slip right out of her head.

''I need to do this, Mattie,'' he said. ''I've been going crazy after weeks in the woods, in that tiny cabin. I told you I came home to find some answers, and I know they'll come. But I can't say when, and I need something to focus my energies on until they do.''

The words seemed to tumble from him, the need for understanding turning his onyx eyes awesomely intense, and before Mattie even realized she'd opened her mouth, before she'd had time to comprehend all the complications this was going to add to her life, she murmured, "Well, I guess it'll be okay."

Before too long, Mattie found herself sitting beside Conner in his pickup truck as they headed for the neighboring town of Mountview, where the nearest lumberyard was located.

In order to give herself time to run a comb through her hair, wash the sleep from her eyes, brush her teeth, not to mention slip on some unmentionables, a fact she hadn't been able to bring herself to mention, Mattie had agreed with Conner's suggestion that he walk back to the cabin to retrieve his truck and then drive back to the inn to pick her up.

Just as she'd promised, Brenda had made herself scarce. Mattie had found mother and son cloistered in the big, airy bedroom upstairs, Scotty watching cartoons and Brenda sitting in a chair, her thoughts miles away.

"I'm going into town," she'd said to Brenda.

The woman had only nodded.

"Do you need anything?" Mattie had asked.

Brenda had sighed and just shaken her head.

Mattie offered Scotty a smile. The poor child had hovered protectively over his mother since their arrival, would hardly leave her side for more than a few moments at a time. He'd witnessed things that no child should, was being forced to grow up way before his time. The youngster should be out playing soccer and baseball, or racing around on a bicycle with friends, not guarding his mother and coming to grips with his disenchantment regarding his father's behavior.

Sometimes life just wasn't fair.

Mattie knew that very, very soon she was going to have to gently suggest that Brenda allow Scotty to go back to school. Both mother and son needed a few days to recoup, but returning to a normal routine would be best for the child.

However, that was a worry to be taken care of tomorrow. Right now Mattie had other concerns on her mind.

She glanced over at Conner as he sat behind the steering wheel, his chin tipped up a fraction, his swarthy complexion regal, his dark gaze on the road. But she knew that beneath that proud profile there was a troubled mind. The plight he found himself in required just as much compassion and understanding as that of the guests she was harboring at Freedom Trail. Granted, Conner wasn't living under the same kind of threat to his physical safety, but he was suffering psychological distress.

She splayed her palm on the smooth leather seat. "Nice truck," she commented.

"Thanks. It's one of an eight-truck fleet."

Mattie smiled. "You own a fleet of trucks?"

She found the sound of Conner's light laughter delightful.

"Don't be too impressed," he told her. "Thunder Contracting offers site managers the use of the trucks for transportation to and from work. My employees see it as a perk for them. I see it as a perk for me."

She nodded, understanding his unspoken words.

"Providing transportation gives your workers one less excuse for not showing up."

"Exactly." After a second, Conner said, "I sure do have a great group of guys working for me. They've kept the business afloat without me for months now."

She silently studied his handsome profile.

"From the second I was slapped with that lawsuit—" he kept his eyes trained on the roadway ahead "—I was overwhelmed with meetings with lawyers, gathering evidence, sitting in the courthouse. It was a nightmare."

His choice of words was ironic, seeing as how one nightmare had provoked another. Evidently he realized it, too—hence the grimace that furrowed his brow when he cast her a quick glance.

"But my men have been great," he continued. "They've kept the contracted jobs going and have even bid on new ones."

"You've been communicating with them?"

"Oh, yes," he said. Then he chuckled again. "I may be living with few creature comforts at the cabin, but I've got my trusty cell phone."

"We'd all be lost without modern technology."

He murmured, "You can say that again."

After that there was a lull in the conversation, and it gave her the chance to ask, "How have you been?"

She knew he would understand the question…that she was asking about the dreams.

His long hair was tucked back behind the ear that faced her, and Mattie imagined herself scooting closer to him, whispering sweet nothings against his warm, corded neck. She remembered how earlier this morning he'd taken a drink from her coffee mug while her fingers were still curled around the heated ceramic. The moment had been deliciously intimate.

"The nightmares are coming less frequently," he said. Then after a short, bewildered pause, he added, "They've changed."

"Changed?" Interest had Mattie's spine straightening.

Conner nodded. "I told you about the heat. And the loud, angry voices. The movement. That I experienced great fear in the dreams." He moistened his lips. "Well, now everything is bathed in white light. I feel...separated from what's taking place rather than being in the midst of it all. I'm no longer participating. I'm more a spectator."

What had happened to cause this change? Mattie wondered. She could plainly see that the same question was running through Conner's thoughts.

"I don't wake up feeling terrified any longer."

"That's a change for the better, I'd say."

He nodded. "But I'm still no closer to discovering what it all means."

Dr. Grey Thunder's words echoed through her mind. *Urge Conner to come visit us. We'd like to see him.*

If she were to mention the doctor, Conner would question her about their affiliation, and that could cause the conversation to get too close to Brenda and Scotty. But she and Conner had already discussed Joseph.

"Conner," she began haltingly, but then boldly blurted, "you need to go see your grandfather."

"No," he said immediately. "That won't help me."

"How do you know?" Before he could answer, she tossed out, "Why have you not gone to see him before this? You've been home for weeks. Have the two of you argued? Did something happen—"

"Nothing happened."

The tone of his voice warned her to probe no further.

Silence.

Conner sighed. "Believe me, Mattie, I didn't fight with my grandfather."

Unable to stop herself, she softly queried, "So why have you not visited him? Why have you stayed away from the reservation? For *years?*"

Braking at the traffic light on the edge of town, he turned to look at her, long and steadily. Finally he said, "I just don't know."

Confusion clouded his raven eyes.

"Go see him," she urged, keeping her voice gentle. "He raised you. He loves you. He might be able to give you some clues about the past. About what the images in your dream mean. And besides all that, he's a shaman, Conner. H-he's very…astute."

Had she said too much? Would Conner ask how she knew of Joseph's perceptive nature?

But Conner seemed too wrapped up in his own problems to ask any questions. He looked out the window and muttered, "I just don't know."

Quickly Mattie offered, "I'll go with you."

His gaze was like a laser beam on her face. He was obviously contemplating why she'd make such an offer.

"I mean it," she said, before he had time to come up with excuses to reject her suggestion. "I'd be happy to go with you. Pick me up tomorrow morning and we'll drive around the lake to the reservation."

Conner searched her face without saying a word. The car behind them honked its horn, alerting him that the light had turned green. He silently drove into the town of Mountview.

Finally impatience got the better of Mattie. "Conner! What do you say? Will you go?"

He nodded slowly. "If you'll go with me."

Triumph ignited happy fireworks in her chest.

Conner dropped Mattie off at Mountview's town hall, where she spent twenty minutes or so filling out the paperwork for a building permit. The clerk told her the permit would be processed in about a week. Mattie wrote the woman a check to pay the fee, and then walked up the block to the combination hardware store and lumberyard, where she'd arranged to meet Conner.

Sunshine warmed the glorious late-October day, and Mattie tipped her face heavenward to soak up the bright rays. Soon winter would cloak New England in a blanket of snow, so she wanted to enjoy this nice weather while she could.

Winter offered many benefits—skiing down the mountainous slopes, snuggling by a roaring fire with a good book clutched in one hand and a cup of cocoa in the other, baking hearty bread on gray afternoons. But Mattie had to admit that she favored any of the three other seasons over winter.

Passing the movie theater, she nodded hello to a stranger on the street.

She was so pleased with herself at the moment. Conner had agreed to visit his grandfather. She could just imagine how happy the elderly shaman would be for the opportunity to spend some time with his grandson.

Mattie was only vaguely aware when she passed the teen who was taping a paper to the glass of the pharmacy's storefront. But seeing Brenda's image staring down at her from the next telephone pole stopped her in her tracks.

"REWARD! Have you seen this woman?"

Her mouth went dry as sand, and she glanced around her covertly before reaching up and snatching the poster off the pole. She turned and saw the teenager attach another poster to a big blue mailbox halfway down the block.

She hurried toward him. "Hey," she called, and he looked up at her. "Can I talk to you a minute?"

The boy nodded and shrugged at the same time, then loped toward her. When he got close enough, Mattie gauged his age to be around thirteen or fourteen.

"What's this?" she asked, pointing to the poster she'd retrieved from the telephone pole.

Again he shrugged. "Dunno. Guess some woman is missing." He scratched at his shoulder. "This guy offered me fifty bucks and his autograph if I'd tape the posters up all over town. Said he was going to be famous and that his autograph was going to be worth a fortune."

Tommie Boy.

The kid's nose scrunched up dubiously. "I didn't really want the guy's autograph, just the money. But he was too big for me to say no, so I took it." He grinned, his face beaming. "I'm going to use the fifty bucks to buy a new skateboard."

"That sounds like fun," Mattie said. Then she asked, "How many posters did the man give you?"

"Not many. Fifteen or so."

Mattie hesitated, then said, "C-could I help you?"

"Thanks, lady, but I only have three left."

"I'll take those," she offered. "Then you can go pick out that skateboard you're wanting."

"Great! Thanks."

The teen handed over the posters and then charged off down the street.

Three from the boy, one from the telephone pole, one on the pharmacy window and one on the mailbox. That meant there were nine more posters to find and get rid of.

Mattie hurried down the street, plucking a poster from the window of the hardware store as she passed. She attempted to be as nonchalant about the chore as she could. Getting noticed was the last thing she wanted. Tommie Boy would probably return to town before too many days passed. Maybe Mattie should suggest to Brenda that it would be safer for her and Scotty to leave the state.

The hunt took her three streets over from where she started before she was satisfied that she'd found all the posters that advertised Brenda's image. Mattie was shaking as she sat down on the bench. Taking a few of the papers at a time, she ripped them in half, then into quarters. When she'd destroyed all the posters, she twisted to toss them into the empty garbage receptacle behind the bench, then turned back around slowly and folded her hands in her lap.

Mattie gulped cool air into her lungs and tried to calm the riot of images floating in her head.

Scotty when he'd arrived on her doorstep, wide-eyed with fear. Brenda with her bruised and gashed face.

Then the impressions pressing in on Mattie changed. The woman's battered face became Susan's. Her sister's pale blue eyes weeping. Her soft voice, bewildered, as she'd begged Mattie for answers, again and again, as to why a husband who was supposed to love her would want to hurt her.

Mattie closed her eyes, and she was drawn five years into the past.

The rosewood casket had a smooth, glossy finish. The brass handles and corner pieces reflected the sunlight from where it sat supported atop the hole in the ground awaiting it.

Grief ripped at Mattie's heart.

It could very well be that the only thing between Brenda and a demise similar to Susan's was Mattie.

What was she doing flirting with the idea of having Conner work on the carriage house while Brenda and Scotty were residing at the inn? Had she totally lost all semblance of her common sense? Hadn't Conner said that he'd have a plumber install the pipes for the bathroom fixtures? Hadn't he mentioned that an electrician would be needed to update the wiring? And hadn't he said that an inspector would have to come for final approval?

With workers coming and going at Freedom Trail,

keeping Brenda's presence a secret would be next to impossible. One of the workers might make an innocent remark to someone in town about Mattie's guests. What if she'd missed one of the reward posters? What if one of them got into the hands of someone who happened to see Brenda at the B and B? Being the root of all evil, cash was simply too much for some people to resist.

But what about Conner and the problems he was facing? The question whispered through her head.

Hadn't she just this morning come to the conclusion that he was in need of understanding and sympathy, too? He'd said he needed something to focus his attention on, something to occupy him, something to deflect his vexing restlessness until he found the answers he sought.

"You, Mattie Russell," she murmured to herself firmly, "have allowed the desires of your body to cloud your thinking."

Conner Thunder was fully capable of solving his own problems. He didn't need her help. Not to the extent that Brenda and Scotty did, anyway.

He had family who cared about him and would be more than happy to be there for him. All he had to do was reach out to them. Brenda didn't have a single soul to rely on but Mattie.

He wasn't in any physical danger. Brenda's very life had been threatened by the man who was supposed to love, honor and cherish her. And she feared the angry, out-of-control boxer enough that she had fled her home with her son despite the serious probability of violent behavior from Tommie Boy that her escape would incite.

Mattie sighed, her shoulders rounding sadly. There was a reason she kept to herself. There was a clear and strong motivation for her solitary lifestyle.

The safety of the women she harbored.

How she had lost sight of that was beyond her.

That wasn't true, she was forced to admit. Not true at all.

She'd let her purpose fall by the wayside because of Conner. Because of the effect he had on her. From their very first meeting.

She'd been mesmerized by every aspect of him. Intrigued by his mysterious dream. Captivated by his good looks. Titillated by the feelings he provoked in her. Delighted with their flirtatious banter. Excited by the prospect of being desired. Enchanted by his touch. Seduced by his kiss.

Even now her heart fluttered against her rib cage and her breathing escalated as she merely thought of him.

Brilliant autumn days such as this one were meant to be savored. They were not meant for discovering that you'd completely lost your senses, that you'd acted like an utter fool due to something as impractical as raging hormones.

Having Conner and a bunch of construction workers renovating the carriage house simply wasn't feasible while Brenda and her son were staying at the B and B. It just wasn't safe for Brenda. Not while Tommie Boy was offering a reward for information on her whereabouts.

Mattie knew the right thing to do—the *only* thing to do—was to put Brenda and Scotty above her own paltry wants.

With a plan now firm in her mind, Mattie scanned the clear skies, her fingers trailing absently down the length of her neck.

But she'd already told Conner he could coordinate the renovation project. How would she ever rationalize her change of mind?

She could explain about her work with abused women. She could tell him about Brenda and Scotty, and the terrifying danger the two would face if their presence at Freedom Trail became known.

Don't tell nobody I'm here. Brenda's inflexible voice rolled into her mind, the woman's huge, terrified eyes haunting her thoughts.

Mattie had promised Brenda she wouldn't expose her. To anyone. And Mattie intended to honor that promise. She'd been working too hard to garner the woman's trust to break it.

She didn't have a doubt that Conner could be trusted with the knowledge—she just had to get Brenda's permission first, that was all. But until she was able to convince Brenda that Conner was trustworthy, how was she going to explain to Conner that she couldn't have anyone working on her property?

Mattie's neck muscles had become so tight that her head had begun to ache at the temples.

She'd just have to find a way. That's all there was to it.

Chapter Five

"So..."

Even though Conner's tone was soft, it made Mattie start with a slight jerk.

"You going to tell me what happened?"

"What happened?" Realizing she sounded like some idiot parrot, she attempted to look as if she were fully cognizant, fully in the moment. But the truth of the matter was, she was preoccupied and had been during the entire drive home.

They were unloading the last of their purchases from the bed of his truck. He carried two gallons of paint into the carriage house. She followed him inside with two more.

Conner set down the paint cans and turned to face her. "Come on, Mattie. It's pretty obvious that something happened between the time I let you off at the town hall and when you met up with me at the store. You've been awfully quiet. Like something is worrying you. Did they give you a hard time at the building department over the permit?''

Of course! The permit. It was the perfect excuse. Why hadn't she thought of it before?

"The permit won't be issued until next week," she told him. "We'll have to put off starting any work until then.''

"Is that what's bothering you? I may not be able to call in the plumber and the electrician until we have a permit number to offer them, but that shouldn't stop me from coming—''

"I'd really rather wait until we have a permit. We're supposed to display it prominently. That's what the clerk told me, anyway.''

"Yes, but—''

"I want to wait," she repeated in a rush.

He just stood there, clearly confused by this sudden brusqueness she was displaying.

The urge to squirm under his scrutiny became more than she could bear. "I have a thousand things I need to do," she blurted out. "If we put off starting the job until next week then…I'll be able to help you." Amazingly, she found her chin dipping toward her chest as she glanced up through raised lashes. "I'm eager to learn some things about…well, you know, about carpentry and painting and hammering…and all that.''

Had that sultry voice come from her throat?

Well, she couldn't have him thinking she was a complete lunatic, could she? She'd accepted his help with the renovation just hours ago and now she was trying to put him off. An excuse to start at a time when she'd be free to help was plausible enough. She didn't want to hurt his feelings, not after he'd gone to all this trouble for her.

But even as she made the silent excuses, she wanted to kick herself for using that coy, please-rescue-me tone. What was she thinking? Hadn't she just decided that she couldn't afford to toy with this flirtation with Conner? That she'd made a choice to dedicate her life to helping women who could not help themselves? That the lives she touched, made better—even saved, in some instances—were worth the isolation she was forced to endure?

It was obvious that he wasn't quite sure what to think of her change of mind. The bewilderment creasing his brow might have made her confess all had she not been in such turmoil.

"Okay, Mattie," he said finally. "We'll do things your way."

He pulled a business card from his back pocket and offered it to her. "This has my cell phone number on it. Call me when you're ready to start the job."

They walked across the lawn to his truck.

"You're not angry, are you?" she felt compelled to ask. "That I want to wait?"

He pulled opened his driver-side door. "I'm not angry. But you should know that, as long you've applied for the permit, it's perfectly acceptable that we can begin work. It's not like federal agents are going to show up at your door, or something."

"I do understand," she said. "And I'll clear my calendar just as quick as I can." Without offering any more, she promised, "I'll call you."

The combination nod and shrug he offered her was

clear indication that he was acquiescing only because she was giving him no other choice. The engine roared to life.

A sudden thought had her calling out his name after he'd backed several feet down her drive. He braked.

Mattie jogged to the truck. "Are we still visiting Joseph tomorrow?"

He hesitated, and the tension she was already feeling increased. Finally he said, "Is ten o'clock good for you?"

"Ten is great," she told him. "I'll be ready."

The instant she saw the elderly shaman's dark eyes light with joy when he looked upon Conner, Mattie knew that every second of awkwardness she'd suffered during the drive over to the reservation had been worth it.

"Conner."

"Grandfather."

The men embraced. Joseph's weathered face nearly crumpled with the deep emotion that obviously pulsed through him. But he held himself together, his eyes glittering with moisture as he smiled over Conner's shoulder at Mattie.

However, the poignant moment didn't last long. Conner's back stiffened. He planted his hands on his grandfather's shoulders and drew away. Mattie could tell he was having a hard time meeting Joseph's gaze.

She suffered a moment of tension as Conner began to explain how he and Mattie had met on the far side of Smoke Lake near her B and B. Conner had no idea about Mattie and Joseph's affiliation, but she needn't have worried. When she'd finally approached Joseph with a request for counseling for the abused women who stayed with her, the shaman had promised never to discuss her work with anyone. He'd been true to his word, infinitely trustworthy, and Mattie knew he wouldn't mention her work, even to his grandson, without first getting an okay from Mattie.

As she'd watched Conner drive away from Freedom Trail yesterday, Mattie had planned to discuss with Brenda her wish to tell Conner about Brenda's presence and all that it meant. Mattie had wanted to set Conner straight about why she couldn't have a bunch of people coming and going when she had someone secreted away at the inn.

However, she'd gone inside to find Scotty hovering over a sobbing and furious Brenda. Apparently the woman had phoned the bank, only to discover that her husband had closed out both their checking and savings accounts, leaving Brenda without a penny to her name.

Earlier, Mattie had tried to get Brenda to at least visit an ATM to retrieve some money for herself, but Brenda hadn't been in any shape to do much more than lie curled in a fetal position and cry. Mattie remembered considering "getting tough" with Brenda, citing Scotty as a motivation for the woman to buck up and pull herself together, but she had decided against it. Brenda wasn't ready for that.

Some women, Mattie had discovered over the years, could be bullied into a strong resolve. Others used anger as a means of getting through the most difficult part of separating from their abusers. Still

others—women like Brenda—had been so beaten
down that they had no self-esteem to speak of. These
woman couldn't take being harassed, even if that ha-
rassment might be for their own good…or the good
of their children. These women needed coddling. At
least for a bit. They needed time to figure out how
their lives had gotten to such a state and what they
were going to do now that they were on their own.

Brenda had spent the day in such turmoil that Mattie hadn't even considered broaching the idea of telling Conner about her and Scotty's presence at the
inn. Instead, Mattie had spent hours assuring Brenda
that she could start over again. That she and Scotty
had a wonderful chance at a new life free from fear
and pain and torment. Once Brenda had calmed
down, she and Mattie had then sat at the kitchen table
and started talking about making some plans that in-
cluded, for starters, a trip to the court for a protective
order against Tommie. Agreeing to such an action
had been a huge step for Brenda.

"Can I offer you both something to drink?"

The shaman's question brought Mattie back to the
present. She said, "No, thank you. I'm fine. In fact,
I was thinking of taking a walk. I saw a produce
stand a couple of blocks up the road." She looked
over at Conner. "Would you mind, Conner? That
way you and your grandfather would have more freedom to, you know, talk…about things."

Conner, she knew without a doubt, possessed a
strong enough character to deal with her bullying him
into discussing his dreams with Joseph. The twinkle
in Conner's onyx gaze told her he was cognizant of
the message she was sending.

"That will be fine," he told her. He walked her to the door. "I'll be sure to talk. About everything."

They shared a smile. Softly she said, "I won't wander far."

The screen door closed behind her and she heard Joseph Thunder say, "Mattie's a special woman."

"Yes, she is," Conner agreed.

A thrill coursed across Mattie's flesh.

It shouldn't matter to her what Conner thought of her. But it did.

She strolled a short distance down the street, stopping at the produce stand. She made small talk with the woman who sat under the awning with a baby cradled against her chest in a special strap that left her arms free so she could accommodate her customers.

The squash looked plump and green and Mattie chose two. The beans were fresh, the last of the crop, she was told, and she asked for a pound, which she decided then and there would be delicious simmered with some leftover ham for dinner.

Mattie watched the woman. Frequently her fingers would trail down the length of her baby's body, smooth over its rounded behind, pat its back. She discovered that her hand had inadvertently found its way to a spot low on her tummy.

Would she ever have a baby to cuddle? Would she ever have—

She blanched, her heart feeling as if it had skipped a couple of beats.

Mattie couldn't remember a time when such thoughts had crossed her mind. Of course, she'd had dolls as a toddler. Her maternal instinct had been developed by playing Mama just like that of millions of other little girls. But those childish fancies had faded into oblivion somewhere along the line.

First she'd run headfirst into puberty. Then she'd galloped through her young adult years, attending community college while at the same time trying to help her aging parents run the inn. She'd begun dreaming of taking over the business someday and had wanted to learn everything she could about the running of Freedom Trail. Then Mattie had witnessed the trauma Susan had experienced: caught in an abusive relationship yet stubbornly determined that there was somehow some way to change her husband into that wonderful knight in shining armor she'd thought him to be prior to marrying him.

Her sister's ordeal had filled Mattie with a kind of hopelessness at first. Her parents, and Mattie, too, had tried to talk sense into Susan. Tried to get her to listen to reason. Tried to get her to separate herself from her husband for good. But Susan would have none of it.

Mattie had experienced resentfulness, too, against her sister. Susan had made the whole family sick with worry. And that hadn't seemed fair to Mattie.

But her sister's tragic death had filled Mattie with a rage she'd never imagined she could feel. And it was that fury that had placed her on the path of getting herself informed about physical and psychological abusers and the people they mistreated, knowledge had helped Mattie immensely. Through educating herself, she was able to help her parents deal with their guilt and grief. Helped them to move on with their lives. Understanding the issues had also

helped Mattie to map out her future. A future of helping abused women. A future that, she'd thought,
didn't have room in it for husbands and babies of
her own…not when she was so busy taking care of
other women and their babies, protecting them from
the battering husbands they had made the terrible
mistake of marrying.

So why now? she wondered. Why would the sight
of this precious infant have her pressing her palm to
her belly? Why had her thoughts turned so wistful
and longing?

Instinct had her gazing back toward Joseph Thunder's brick bungalow. Her brows rose in surprise
when she saw Conner walking toward her. After paying the woman for her produce purchases and bid-
ding her good day, Mattie went to meet Conner.

"You didn't stay very long." She couldn't keep
the comment from spilling from her.

Conner's only answer was a shrug.

"Conner," she said, her tone pressing, "you
haven't seen your grandfather in years. You should
have been there all morning and into the afternoon."

"I couldn't very well do that with you waiting,
now, could I?"

Aghast, Mattie's mouth opened. "Don't use me as
an excuse—"

Conner laughed. "It is just too easy to get you
riled. Look, Mattie, Grandfather has some things to
do. We plan to meet again, okay?"

Satisfied with his answer, she smiled and nodded.
"Did you tell him? About your dreams?"

They walked down the street together back toward
Conner's truck.

"Yes," he said. "But I don't know what good it did. Grandfather offered me no answers."

This surprised Mattie. She knew Joseph to be almost uncannily knowing, a person who had an eerie sense of understanding about a person's problem and the root of it almost before any talking had been done. And as a shaman, Joseph had a responsibility to offer advice to those who came to him seeking it.

In the past, Mattie had seen Joseph counsel the women who stayed with her, with amazing results. He had a way of making a person see her life clearly. If a person understood her past, she'd heard Joseph often say, then she could better see where she wanted to go in the future.

"But he did offer me this." Conner held up a plain brown paper sack. "It's an herb meant to induce a deep sleep," he continued. "And vivid dreams. Grandfather feels that maybe this will help me to focus in on what's happening in my dream. To better decipher the meaning."

They reached the back of the truck and moved along the passenger side. Evidently Conner meant to open her door for her. Mattie couldn't help but think that was sweet of him.

"So are you glad you came to see Joseph?" she asked.

As she asked the question, Conner opened her door. She made to climb into the cab, but he stopped her, his fingers warm on her forearm.

"What I'm glad about—"

In a heartbeat, the air thickened and heated, and Mattie got the sense that the autumnal sun had shifted in the sky to a spot directly overhead. That it shone down on them, its concentrated rays heating the space right where they stood to an unbearable temperature.

"—is that you're with me this morning."

The husky quality of his voice sent shivers skittering throughout her body like the warm spray of an unexpected rainstorm. A vague thought that he was once again avoiding Joseph as a topic of conversation hovered at the edges of her brain, but she gazed up into his face—took in the intensity of his expression—and the hazy notion fluttered away.

With the backs of his fingers he grazed a gentle trail up her jawline, then smoothed his thumb over the curve of her ear. She was only barely able to stifle the shudder that threatened to rumble forth from her very bones.

Sudden hunger made her blood slog through her veins.

She shouldn't...

She shouldn't...

The muddled thought echoed, ricocheting in the strange empty chaos that had assailed her mind. Her thoughts were an odd mixture of blankness and disarray.

There was something she shouldn't do, but before she could figure out what it was she'd become completely lost in the mesmerizing depths of his black-as-coal eyes, in the compelling aura that was Conner's alone, in the titillating prospect that his lips might press to hers.

Oh, how she wished they would.

And they did.

His mouth crushed against hers in a kiss that could

only be described as soul satisfying. Hot. Sweet. Luscious. Mind numbing.

Conner pulled back, his gaze powerful. He tucked curled fingers under her chin, dragged the pad of his thumb over her moist bottom lip. The heady desire etched in every sharp angle of his face made Mattie's heart pound furiously.

"Whatever happens with all this," he whispered, "whether I find answers to my questions or not, I do know one thing. I feel blessed by The Great One to have met you."

They shared one last, long look, and then Conner inched back so she could slide into the passenger seat of the truck. The door slammed shut...and Mattie's mind cleared.

In an instant she remembered what it was she shouldn't do.

And why.

The ax sank into the log with a satisfying thwack. Chips went flying, and Conner loosened the blade from the wood with a firm twist before raising the ax above his head and swinging it down again. This time the blade cut through, and the chunks of timber tumbled several feet apart. He set down the ax, retrieved the wood and placed the cut pieces on the neat stack he was making.

The cabin was there for the tribe's use. Anyone could stay for as long as they liked, but the Kolheek way was to leave the place as you'd found it. The chilly mornings had forced Conner to light a fire in the woodstove, so he was replacing the firewood he'd used over the past weeks.

GET FREE BOOKS and a FREE GIFT WHEN YOU PLAY THE...

SLOT MACHINE GAME!

Just scratch off the silver box with a coin. Then check below to see the gifts you get!

YES! I have scratched off the silver box. Please send me the 2 free Silhouette Romance® books and gift for which I qualify. I understand I am under no obligation to purchase any books, as explained on the back of this card.

315 SDL DRRE

215 SDL DRRU
(S-R-02/03)

FIRST NAME	LAST NAME

ADDRESS

APT.#	CITY

STATE/PROV.	ZIP/POSTAL CODE

7 7 7 Worth TWO FREE BOOKS plus a BONUS Mystery Gift!

Worth TWO FREE BOOKS!

Worth ONE FREE BOOK!

TRY AGAIN!

Visit us online at www.eHarlequin.com

DETACH AND MAIL CARD TODAY!

The Silhouette Reader Service™ — Here's how it works:

Accepting your 2 free books and gift places you under no obligation to buy anything. You may keep the books and gift and return the shipping statement marked "cancel." If you do not cancel, about a month later we'll send you 6 additional books and bill you just $3.34 each in the U.S., or $3.80 each in Canada, plus 25¢ shipping & handling per book and applicable taxes if any.* That's the complete price and — compared to cover prices of $3.99 each in the U.S. and $4.50 each in Canada — it's quite a bargain! You may cancel at any time, but if you choose to continue, every month we'll send you 6 more books, which you may either purchase at the discount price or return to us and cancel your subscription.

*Terms and prices subject to change without notice. Sales tax applicable in N.Y. Canadian residents will be charged applicable provincial taxes and GST.

Although the day was cool, the sun's rays knifing down through the trees combined with the arduous task of cutting the wood had forced him to tug off his shirt. He swiped his forearm across his brow and then set another large piece of wood up onto the huge old tree trunk, hacked and nicked with what seemed to be thousands of ax marks.

He arched the ax up high, but the rustle he heard in the brush had him relaxing his shoulder muscles, the steel head of the ax coming to rest on the mossy ground.

Sunlight glinted golden against Mattie's long flaxen hair, and Conner felt his very soul sing at the sight of her.

He hadn't been able to figure out this complex woman. She held an overwhelming allure for him, and had since their very first meeting. He got the impression—no, he pretty much was certain—that she felt the same about him. There was something almost mystical about the fascination they found in one another.

However, Mattie seemed to run hot and cold. She'd allow herself to dabble in the fine art of flirtation one moment—and quite frankly, it was a pastime she was rather adept at—but the next minute she'd seem aloof, as if she were doing all she could to restrain the desires she so obviously felt.

"Hi," she called out to him.

He lifted a hand in silent greeting, then automatically reached for his T-shirt and pulled it on.

"I was taking a walk." She paused several feet from him. "I heard the chopping. And was curious." Her eyes slid away from his face.

There it was again. That distancing dance she performed. Conner got the sense that she wanted to seek him out, yet at the same time she didn't. As if she were enticed and intrigued by the idea of waltzing with him, but for some reason she felt that enjoying the music and the movement was off-limits.

"Just cutting some firewood," he explained.

She nodded. When she took her bottom lip between her teeth, Conner was reminded how lusciously sweet her honeyed mouth had tasted.

"So…how have you been?" Between her fingers she twirled a long piece of wild grass that she'd evidently plucked from somewhere alongside the path that had brought her to him.

I've been going out of my mind waiting for you to call, a silent voice intoned. But rather than expressing that thought, he found himself being just as honest on another subject altogether.

"I've been feeling a little under the weather today."

He didn't know what it was about Mattie that invited a person to unload his problems, but he realized that every time he was with her he ended up unburdening himself.

Mattie moved closer, a silent invitation for him to expand on whatever might be bothering him.

Dark emotions rushed up to engulf him, causing him to regret opening this can of worms. He sighed.

"I've been wondering," he began haltingly, "why Kit-tan-it-to'wet would allow such bad fortune to befall one person while good fortune is bestowed on another."

Bewilderment shadowed her deep blue eyes, and Conner felt compelled to explain further.

"Why would the Great Father condemn one man to a wheelchair for the remainder of his life and leave me strong and whole?"

Understanding dawned, lightening her gaze. She moved close enough that he could smell her warm, fresh-rain scent. "People have wondered for thousands of years why bad things happen to certain people and not to others. I guess it's just not meant for us to know everything."

He realized what she said was true, but the cloud that had descended on him didn't lift.

"Conner, from everything you've said about the accident, you have nothing to feel guilty about. You cannot hold yourself responsible for the irresponsible acts of others."

This, too, was true. He moistened his lips, remaining silent.

Mattie was inches from him now and she reached out, her fingers creamy-pale against his swarthy skin. The contrast affected him and he couldn't seem to take his eyes from the spot where their flesh made contact.

Evidently unaware of what her nearness was doing to him, she softly whispered, "You were cleared by the courts of any wrongdoing. You told me so yourself. You have nothing to feel guilty about. Cut yourself some slack, Conner. The judge cleared you. Now you need to clear yourself. Forgive yourself."

She meant only to console him, he understood that. But the attraction that sucked him into a vacuum each and every time he was with Mattie pulled and tugged at him now. He was in clear danger of succumbing to its lure yet again.

The magnetic energy that swirled at ever-increasing speeds and threatened to bring him to his knees was so strong that she couldn't help but perceive it. Her gaze darkened to a rich sapphire as the animation in her facial muscles eased into a different kind of intensity. Her breath quickened, her full, rounded breasts rising and falling more noticeably.

Then she did the most extraordinary thing. She slid her fingers from his forearm, balled her hand into a fist and pressed it tight to her diaphragm. She swallowed, and although she didn't actually step away from him, her body eased back.

The resulting space was all that Conner needed. He inhaled deeply. Exhaled. And then he shook his head as he emitted a nearly inaudible chuckle.

"Thanks," he told her.

Her expression was inscrutable.

"I don't know what that is," he continued. "But every time I'm with you my head gets so clogged up with it that I just can't think."

Mattie remained silent, her blue eyes pensive.

"It's pretty clear that there's something between us...some powerful force that just becomes...overwhelming." His thoughts and words were coming slowly, but he pressed on. "It's also obvious to me that, although you've been tempted a time or two by this...thing, these feelings that swoop down on us, you have some reason for wanting to avoid it."

While he was terribly curious about the motivation behind her desire to evade the very physical and emotional attraction between them, he felt obliged to speak his mind about these encounters.

Before she could respond, he added, "I'd like to avoid it, too."

Her blue eyes widened, making it plain that this wasn't what she'd expected to hear from him.

He'd given this matter much thought over the past few days.

"I've spent my whole life shying away from relationships," he admitted. "Don't get me wrong. I've dated. I've enjoyed plenty of friendships with women. But the moment things become intense, I turn tail and run."

The contemplative emotion that had flattened her gaze faded, replaced by a cautious curiosity.

"I can't really tell you why." He realized in that instant that he was being entirely truthful with her. He shrugged. "It could be because I equate serious bonds...relationships...with grief. Let's face it, my mom died when I was a baby, and my dad was never the same. He died when I was six. I've faced the deaths of an aunt and two uncles, as well. And I told you at dinner how my other aunt left the reservation, taking her daughter with her. None of us have seen Aunt Holly or Alisa since. Alisa would be in her early twenties now."

He hadn't realized the far-off quality of his voice as he contemplated his past.

"But—" Mattie frowned "—your aunt just up and..."

"Left behind two sons that she never bothered to contact," Conner filled in. "Tristin and Eli. That family was completely split apart. I guess you could say that the whole Thunder clan has been devastated by loss and grief.''

After a short pause he said, ''I guess what I'm trying to say is that I appreciate your strength. Several times you've put a stop to…well, that allure, that force, or whatever that seems to knock me off balance.''

He wished he could find the right words to better clarify his thoughts.

''I don't feel whole, Mattie,'' he told her. ''I'm not sure I ever will.'' Then he added, ''I've had enough sorrow. I don't ever want to care about someone to the point that losing them will cause me pain.''

As he talked, the interest on her face had become keener. Now that he'd gone silent, she studied him.

Absently she grasped the stem end of the blade of grass between thumb and index finger and pulled it through her fingers of the opposite hand. ''Conner, I do understand that you've experienced an inordinate amount of loss in your family.'' She stopped long enough to take a breath. ''But…I think that grief is a fact of life that all of us have to contend with at some time or other. I know I have. In fact, I don't know anyone who hasn't been touched in some way by death. But that shouldn't turn you against finding a loving relationship. There's nothing so bad that it should keep you from finding a mate. Settling down. Being happy with…someone.''

There was an odd hitch in her voice, Conner noticed. It was almost as if she were trying to convince him of something she wasn't quite sure of herself.

The very notion had his mouth spreading into a slow smile.

"Well, something's happened to turn you against loving relationships," he observed.

She chuckled then. "Oh, trust me, I'm a firm believer in love. But the rules don't apply to me." In a rush, she added, "Besides, we were talking about you. I can't help but wonder if everything you're experiencing, all these feelings you're dealing with, aren't somehow tied to the dream you've been having. Did you use the herb your grandfather gave you?"

Conner had been more than a little intrigued by her statement regarding herself and "the rules," but he was forced to answer Mattie's question.

"I haven't," he told her. Then he found himself swallowed up by some monstrous gloom. He scrubbed at his temples. "I...I have to admit that I'm—" Reality sliced through his words, cutting them to the quick.

Gently she supplied, "Scared? Are you afraid of what you might discover? That would be perfectly understandable, you know."

Oh, Great Spirit above, how could this woman read him so well?

"The only way you're going to get the answers you're looking for," she said, "is to face the fear. Face the truth. Face that dream."

Chapter Six

Anxiety pumped through Conner's veins like icy acid as he stalked along the forest path, oblivious to the glorious foliage glinting colorfully in the sunlight, the birds that sang from the branches overhead, the freshness that snapped in the autumn air around him. He had one thought in his mind, and one thought alone: finding Mattie.

Being strapped shirtless to a termite mound couldn't be as torturous as the agitation that surged through his being. He took the front steps two at a time, raised his hand and knocked on the door. And when she didn't open up as quickly as he'd have liked, he banged a second time.

The curtain fluttered and just a moment later the door opened.

"Conner."

Clearly, Mattie was surprised to see him. Somewhere in the back of his brain he vaguely registered the tremendous relief in her expression. That should have given him reason to pause, but he was too distressed at the moment.

"Do you know what time it is?"

"It's early," he admitted bluntly and without apology. He felt more distracted than ever before, but he *was* aware that she was cinching up a white robe—he'd have had to have been made of granite not to notice.

"I need to talk. Now." He shifted his weight, eager to go inside and settle down where they could be comfortable.

But Mattie evidently had another idea. She stepped out onto the porch and pulled the door closed behind her.

"Let's take a walk," she told him, her tone the epitome of tranquillity. "It's a beautiful morning."

This was why he'd sought her out, he guessed. Her uncanny ability to remain calm no matter what was thrown at her.

She went down the steps in front of him, lifted her face to the sunshine and smiled. It was a purely instinctive response, he could tell, like breathing or reaching to pet a furry puppy. You didn't think about it, you just did it.

With her chin tipped upward, her lush locks tumbled down her back in a white-gold cascade, and Conner discovered that just looking at her was soothing to his soul, to his troubled mind.

Mattie looked up at him.

"Conner?"

He blinked, realizing that he hadn't left the spot next to the front door. Feeling like an idiot, he hurried down the stairs and fell into step beside her, his agitation returning full force.

"It's not a dream," he blurted. "It's not something made up by my subconscious. It's…it's a memory."

She looked thoughtful. "So you've recalled something from your past?"

Frustration made him grimace. "No." He heaved a sigh. "The images still aren't completely clear, but…"

Her blue gaze was steady on him. "You used the herb Joseph gave you?"

Conner nodded. "But kava-kava is mild. Helps to bring a deep sleep. It's not strong enough to manipulate the mind."

"So what's made you decide that the dream is a memory?"

"Well…my whole perspective has changed. Remember how I told you that, rather than actually being part of what's happening, I'm standing on the sidelines watching the action?" His gaze searched the air, his hand waving distractedly as he attempted to find the words to describe it all. "That I'm…protected? By this amazing film. A light. A—" he shook his head "—netting that glows."

It sounded silly as he attempted to verbalize what he experienced during the dream, and he felt embarrassed all of a sudden. But when he glanced over at Mattie, she didn't look the least bit skeptical.

"Yes, you did tell me." Then she asked, "But did the herb help at all?"

"I think so. Although none of the images are crystal clear yet," he told her, "I *was* able to make out the voices. One belonged to my father. The other was Joseph's."

His gaze dipped to the curve of her shoulder and he saw then that the robe he'd thought was plain white was, in reality, studded with pale blue flower buds. Hundreds of them covered the soft, satiny fabric.

Moistening his bottom lip, Conner willed himself to avert his eyes, but his gaze continued to roam. It was impossible to miss the way the satin hung over her high, perky breasts. The outlines of her dark nipples were unmistakable against the white material.

"And the fact that you recognized these voices," she continued, seemingly oblivious to his too-intimate scrutiny, "is what has you thinking that this was an event that actually took place sometime during your childhood?"

He nodded silently.

Her beautiful face lit with excitement. "Conner! If Joseph is in the dream, then he had to have been present when the incident occurred. Go see him. Ask him. He'll be able to tell you—"

"I'm not going to see him." He could feel the scowl that furrowed his brow, that took control of his whole face. "I'm not going to see him ever again, Mattie."

She stopped suddenly and turned to face him, her incredulity apparent in the way she plunked one fisted hand on her hip and asked, "Well, why not?"

He'd expected her to at least try to understand, but instead she was attacking him with this overwhelming amazement that made him think she'd decided he'd gone daft. His irritation flared.

"I already told you," he said. "I heard the voices. Made out a snippet of the angry fight between my father and grandfather."

Even now in his mind's eye he could make out the angry bear figure, waving its massive, sharp-clawed paws in the air.

"'Get out,' he shouted," Conner relayed to Mattie, his gaze fixed on the horizon. "'Leave Smoke Valley and don't come back.'"

The pain that seared into his chest, into his heart, was nearly more than he could bear. He leveled his troubled gaze onto Mattie's face.

"Grandfather took my father away from me," he said, his tone raspy with the anger that engulfed him. "Who does he think he is? He can't manipulate people like that! He can't make those kinds of decisions for people. He stole away those last few precious months I could have had with my dad before he was killed. It wasn't right, Mattie. It wasn't fair!"

"Wait just a minute."

The annoyance he heard in Mattie's voice made him pause. Sure enough, her blue eyes were narrowed, her shoulders square with the tension building inside her.

"You can't say for certain that that's what happened," she said. "You told me that you heard 'a snippet' of what was being said. You can't take a piece of information out of context and form a bunch of ridiculous notions about it." She gulped in a breath. "I won't stand here and let you make half-baked insinuations about a man who is as good-hearted as Joseph Thunder."

"Good-hearted?" He couldn't believe his ears.

"Why are you defending him? Didn't you hear what I said?"

"I heard every word you said." She crossed her arms over her chest. "But you obviously didn't hear what I said. You're too busy making up stories about what those images in your head might mean, when what you should be doing is talking to the one person who might just be able to set you straight." The bark of laughter she emitted was harsh. "Conner Thunder, I don't believe you're at all interested in the truth."

He was seething, and although he knew his anger was focused on his grandfather, he couldn't help the fact that the roiling emotion was getting mixed up in his conversation with Mattie.

"I'll tell you what the truth is," he said. "I've been angry with Joseph for years. It's why I haven't come home to the rez. It's why I found excuses not to help with the construction of the community center last year. Somewhere buried was the memory that Joseph is the reason my father left Smoke Valley. For some reason, the incident became obscured, lost in my brain. But now it's out in the open where everyone can see it in the clear light of day."

Her chin tipped up stubbornly. "Nothing is clear, Conner. You need to stop blaming Joseph and start working on discovering why you buried the truth. And you also need to uncover the rest of the details. Because the Joseph I know would never knowingly hurt a fly, let alone a grandson he loves beyond reason."

Conner glared at her for a long moment. She spoke as if she knew his grandfather well, and some silent inner voice told him this was significant. But he felt too betrayed, too furious to question it.

"I can't believe," he finally said, "that I came to you looking for understanding. Looking for help."

The obstinate shadow that darkened her gaze didn't let up. "I want to understand you, Conner. I want to help you, too. But I can't help a man who refuses to help himself."

She hadn't raised her tone, hadn't shouted or railed. In fact, her voice had remained quiet even as she'd given her opinion.

For the span of many seconds they squared off, their gazes clashing, neither backing down. In the end, the feeling of being let down by her became more than he could take and he turned on his heel and walked away.

Wednesday of the following week, the building permit arrived in a large manila envelope and sat unopened on the hall table. Oh, she knew it was there. Knew she would need to hire a carpenter if she was ever going to start the carriage-house renovation. But she was too busy dealing with Brenda to give the project much thought.

Although Mattie spent the majority of her time simply listening to the woman, Brenda also needed to be taught some basic life skills—keeping a checkbook and savings account, devising a budget. Brenda also needed guidance in dressing for and conducting herself during a job interview.

Mattie stared at the tabletop. Next to the envelope from the building department was another piece of mail. One she had opened. The invitation was covered in romantic white roses. Lori and Grey were having a party.

The couple had married quickly, with no chance of sharing their day with friends. Now that they were in love, they wanted to celebrate. Mattie wasn't sure she could attend. Again, the needs of Brenda and Scotty had to take precedence over a night of fun with her friends.

On a good note, Brenda had made great strides. She was feeling emotionally stronger and much more optimistic about her and her son's future these days. She and Mattie had discussed getting Brenda into some kind of training that would better prepare her for the employment market. And Mattie had even convinced the woman to see a lawyer about filing for divorce.

However, all that had changed after the call Brenda had made this morning.

"I thought we'd agreed," Mattie gently scolded the woman, "that you wouldn't contact anyone while you were working things out."

"I know." Apology was thick in Brenda's tone. "But I was feeling so alone."

Mattie offered a sympathetic smile. "I understand. Really I do. But I'm sure I don't have to remind you about the need for discretion. You haven't wanted me to tell a single soul you're here."

"Sheila won't tell anyone I called her. And I didn't tell her where I am."

"That's good." Mattie took Brenda's hand and gave it a squeeze. "I am glad you called your friend…and not your husband."

"You don't need to worry over that," Brenda said.

"Me and Tommie Boy are through. I'm finished being his punchin' bag."

The resolve in the woman's voice pleased Mattie. Brenda was well on her way to becoming a survivor of domestic abuse.

Some ominous emotions clouded Brenda's plain features. "After talking to Sheila, I do have to admit that I'm scared all over again."

Mattie waited patiently for Brenda to explain.

"Tommie went to see Sheila," she said. "Scared her half crazy, he did. He went over there rantin' and ravin'. He even threatened her. Sheila told me she was sure he was going to hit her."

Brenda paused, her fingers absently rising to the still-healing wound on her temple. When she continued, her words were a mere whisper, "She said Tommie means to hurt me bad when he finds me. He's been promising that to everyone who will listen." Her gaze went fearful. "He means it, Mattie. He'd kill me if he thought he could get away with it. And with that oily manager he's got who seems willing to pour good money after bad, Tommie just might *could* get away with it."

Despite her poor grammar, Brenda's meaning couldn't have been more clear.

"I wish—" her gaze became dreamy, wistful "—I could take Scotty and go far away."

Mattie studied her, from the scabbed-over gash on her face to the pale yellow bruises around her eyes to the tape across her nose. The woman was too young to have been through hell and back. But hell was exactly what she'd experienced being married to a man prone to violence.

Finally Mattie quietly said, "You can do that, Brenda. And I can help you. If that's really what you want to do, I can make the arrangements. Get you and Scotty new identities. I know people who would be willing to help you. People who are far away. I've done it before for women who felt they had no other alternative."

Interest perked Brenda's brows.

"But I do have to warn you," Mattie said, "that kind of life is hard. You can't go back home. Ever. You can't speak to family or friends. You've got to leave everything and everyone behind." She let the idea of it sink in. Softly but firmly she added, "It would be very hard."

"Harder than what I already been through?" Emotion made Brenda's eyes glitter. "Harder than getting banged up every time something don't go right for my husband? Harder than getting my arm broke? My fingers? My jaw? Harder than hiding with Scotty in the darkness of a closet so many times that I done lost count? I want to start fresh. Me and my son deserve to start over."

Knowing this wasn't a decision to be made lightly, or one that should be made when emotions ran high, Mattie patted Brenda's arm and said, "I want you to take some time to think about this."

"I don't need to think. I been thinkin' long enough. I want you to arrange for me to leave Vermont. I want to leave New England. I'll go anywhere, Mattie. California. Alaska. Timbuktu. Anywhere that me and Scotty will be safe."

For a long moment Mattie sat quiet. Then she nodded. "I can have you and Scotty on your way in a couple of days."

For the first time since Brenda had arrived, her posture seemed to ease...and something...what was that—

Mattie's heart wrenched.

Hope. That was hope giving Brenda's eyes a new illumination.

This, Mattie realized, was the best part of her job. Seeing women who arrived on her doorstep, beaten down with defeat and despair, come to life with a newfound optimism for a bright tomorrow.

Brenda blinked, reaching out and touching Mattie on the sleeve. "That man of yours," she began. "I haven't seen him come around." Her tone softened with regret as she asked, "You missed out on him, didn't you? Because of me. I wouldn't let you tell him about me and Scotty being here."

The smile Mattie attempted felt flat, but she hadn't expected Brenda to bring up Conner as a topic of discussion. She hadn't been prepared.

She'd been terribly upset by the conclusions Conner had come to, impulsive assumptions made without all the facts. She'd fretted over it ever since. But her worrying wasn't going to help him any.

Mattie had spoken the truth to him. She'd wanted to help. But she couldn't if he wasn't willing to talk to Joseph, to discover the truth from the only living person able to offer it. But Conner's eyes had hardened with flinty determination when he said he never planned to see his grandfather again.

Idiot man.

Inhaling a steady breath, Mattie said to Brenda, "I

didn't miss out on anything. And I don't want you thinking I did.''

"Well, somebody's losing out on something."

Mattie's forehead creased.

Brenda said, "I peeked out the window when the two of you were talking out back by the building. And again the morning you were walking down the front lane. That man about ate you up with his eyes."

"Oh, stop." Mattie stood up. She didn't want to talk about this. But pride alone had her stating, "You can't miss out on something that was never meant to be in the first place."

She made some inane excuse that allowed her to leave the room, but not before she saw the dubious reflection in Brenda's eyes...and not before she identified the emotion that rolled through her as she voiced those words.

Desolation.

Mattie scanned the rack in the small pharmacy and chose a bottle of shampoo, one of conditioner, a tube of toothpaste, an unscented deodorant and a bar of soap, all in small, travel-sized containers.

She usually frequented the large grocery store located in the town of Mountview, but she'd visited Joseph Thunder to ask if he'd meet Brenda for a counseling session before the woman left town. To save time, Mattie had decided to pick up a few things for Brenda's impending trip right here at Smoke Valley Reservation.

The small string of bells attached to the front door of the shop tinkled, and Mattie lifted her head automatically. Her gaze connected with Conner's and her lips parted in surprise. Luckily she was able to contain the gasp that had gathered in the back of her throat.

Clearly, Conner was just as taken aback by this unexpected encounter as she.

Should she greet him? Ignore him? Or what?

He had been terribly angry with her the last time they'd been together, the morning he'd sought her out to tell her that his dream was a childhood memory. And she'd practically told him that she'd thought his stubborn refusal to talk to his grandfather was just plain stupid.

Mattie resolved to let Conner decide. If he wished to take no notice of her, then she'd follow suit.

A second ticked by, then another, and she could feel her heartbeat pound in her ears. She realized that if he walked away without acknowledging her, she'd be crushed.

He stepped inside the shop, letting the door drift closed behind him. Vaguely she was aware of the tinkling of metal against glass. With his eyes riveted to hers, he made his way toward her.

Relief flooded her in a torrent. She refused to allow herself to examine what that might mean. She didn't want to know.

Then he was close enough that she could feel the heat of him, smell the pine scent that clung to his hair, to his clothes.

"Hi," he said.

He didn't smile. But there wasn't anything antagonistic in his greeting, either. Mattie got the impression that he was as unsure about this meeting as she was.

"I'm surprised you're here." The words left her mouth with no conscious thought. "On the rez, I mean. I thought you were avoiding this place."

His mouth pulled into a grin. "I have been. But I wanted to visit my cousin. Grey just got married not too long ago, and I wanted to meet his new wife."

"Lori." Thinking of her friend, Mattie smiled. "She's a friend of mine. I was her maid of honor when she married Grey."

The troubled look that darkened Conner's features made her feel as if she might have revealed too much. She pressed her lips together in an effort to shut herself up.

After a moment, Conner nodded toward the items she had stacked in the small red plastic basket hanging from her arm.

"You going on a trip?"

She looked down at the toothpaste, the soap and the other products. Then she tipped up her chin. "No," she answered him honestly. "I'm not going anywhere."

He seemed to be waiting for her to elaborate on all those travel-sized purchases she'd chosen, but she remained mulishly silent.

Conner's gaze dipped to the floor. "Look, Mattie," he said, catching her gaze once again, "I'm sorry that I was so…harsh the last time we spoke. This is my problem. It has nothing to do with you and I shouldn't be taking my frustration out on you."

The apology touched her heart. "I know this is something you need to work out, Conner. I'm sorry I butted my nose in. I have no business offering you advice. But I only pushed so hard because—"

I care. Those were the words she'd been about to utter. Luckily she'd stopped herself.

I do care, a quiet voice earnestly intoned from somewhere in the back of her mind. But she dared not admit that. Not if she were to keep her heart safe.

"Because I think it's…that it's very important for you to find the answers you need."

She felt weak in the knees all of a sudden. The longer she stood here, the more she was coming to understand just how much Conner had come to mean to her. She wanted him to be happy and whole. She wanted those nightmares to stop plaguing him. She wanted…

"So," he said, his voice soft, "we're okay? You're not angry with me?"

Mattie shook her head. "I'm not angry."

"Good."

That mysterious allure snaked around their ankles, slowly twisted its way around them, meandering between and about them like a live entity. Conner was cognizant of it. Mattie read it in his intense black gaze.

"Are you going to Grey and Lori's party tonight?"

"I, um, I'm not sure yet."

Conner smiled, and she realized how much she'd missed seeing it.

"I thought you said you were Lori's maid of honor," he said. "I can't believe you'd miss this party."

She smiled, but didn't respond.

"I could pick you up," he pressed.

"Thanks, but—" she shook her head "—I'm really not sure about my plans."

The allure thickened to a density that was becoming awkward.

Finally he said, "I've been waiting for that call you promised."

The remark and his pseudo-hangdog expression called for a smile. The moment was so intense, though, that smiling was difficult for her.

"I wasn't sure you'd still be interested in helping me with the carriage house."

"Of course I am. Has the permit arrived?"

"It has." She shifted the basket, a corporeal reminder of why she had to keep him and everyone else away from Freedom Trail. "But I need another day or two, Conner. Then I'll be ready for you."

He looked at her hard, as though he were searching for some hidden—deeper—meaning in her words. The oxygen seemed to thicken and Mattie felt the need to get out into the fresh air.

"I don't understand why you keep putting me off, Mattie."

Oh, Lord, she wanted to tell him everything. She'd love to reveal everything about her work at Freedom Trail. But with Brenda's decision to go underground came a heavy responsibility. Mattie could not tell anyone what she was planning. She hadn't even told Joseph, a man who'd been helping her for quite some time. Brenda trusted her, and the woman deserved the confidentiality that Mattie had promised.

After Brenda and Scotty were on their way to their new home, then Mattie could come clean with

Conner. She could tell all as soon as her guests were gone.

Mattie sighed. "I do have your number, Conner," she assured him. "I will call you."

That was a promise she had every intention of keeping.

Chapter Seven

When Mattie didn't answer the door the second time he knocked, Conner went around to the back of the inn in search of her. Excitement had him feeling buoyant. The promise in her tone when they had parted this morning had churned him up. He'd begun thinking about the project they would soon start. And he'd drawn up plans for the carriage house.

He had two ideas, actually. He'd sketched out two renditions of the renovations he'd seen in his mind's eye. One utilized only the existing space, the other would necessitate a small addition being built off the back.

The second idea was what had him so energized. With just a small eight-foot extension, he'd added a sitting area and a kitchenette that would allow Mattie's newlywed guests some real privacy. What man and woman who were just starting out and getting to know each other wouldn't like the opportunity of taking their meals alone, in the comfortable seclusion of their own little suite?

Conner grinned, sure that Mattie was going to flip over his idea.

He knew she was too busy to start the work for a couple of days. She'd said as much. And he didn't intend to take up much of her time. All he wanted to do was hand her the plans, and then he'd go on his way.

He walked toward the detached garage, but since it had no windows, he couldn't tell if her car was inside. The yard was empty, and he wondered if she were out by the lake.

Movement in his peripheral vision had his head jerking up toward the house. A curtain had flicked in an upstairs window—Conner was certain of it.

Did Mattie have guests staying at Freedom Trail? Was that why she'd put him off for yet another couple of days, even though, as she'd told him, the building permit had arrived?

But if that were the case, why hadn't she simply said that? Having paying visitors was a perfectly viable excuse for avoiding construction noise that might have people complaining, or worse yet, taking their business elsewhere.

When he'd talked with Mattie in the pharmacy earlier today, she'd shelved the renovation with such a vague reason that he couldn't even remember what it had been...or if she'd even offered one at all.

Conner lifted his face toward the inn's second floor. Was that a shadow falling across the curtain? Was someone up there watching him?

He stared hard, but the form was gone.

There was something furtive about this... something—

A rumble of laughter shook his shoulders. "Conner, old buddy," he murmured to himself, "you've been spending too much time alone. Your imagination is running wild."

The sound of tires crunching on gravel made him swivel his head. Mattie's little compact eased up the long lane, stopping just a couple of yards from him. Tension marred her beautiful face as she opened the door and got out of the car.

"What are you doing here, Conner?" she asked.

He should have been put off by her tone, but his enthusiasm over the plans he'd brought made him oblivious to her mood.

"I've brought you something." He knew there was a zest in his voice she couldn't miss. As he approached her he held out the sheets of graph paper on which he'd drafted the drawings.

She took them from him, and his gaze darted to the large items on the back seat of her car.

"You sure you're not going anywhere?" he asked, indicating the two suitcases with the price tags still affixed to them.

"Just doing a little shopping." She didn't look up, just studied the pages he'd given her.

Then he noticed the gaily wrapped package on the seat. "You've decided to go to Grey and Lori's party?" Although he tried not to feel offended by her declining his offer to take her this evening, he would have been lying if he'd said he wasn't affected.

"I'm still not sure I can," she said in a rush. "I

hope to make an appearance. But even if I do, I won't be able to stay long.''

An awkward moment passed, then she looked up from the plans. ''These are great, Conner. Thanks. I like the one with the addition a lot. It's perfect. Just what I've been looking for all along.''

He smiled, pleased with the notion that he'd been right about which draft she'd choose. ''I thought you'd like it.''

Their gazes locked then, and Conner had the over-whelming sense that Mattie's mind was weighed down with something.

''What is it? What's bothering you, Mattie?''

He made to move toward her, to reach out to her, but she balked. Her hands drew back and she pressed the sheets of paper to her chest in her effort to retreat from him without actually stepping backward.

Startled by her reaction, he let his hand drop to his side. A frown rutted his brow. ''You told me at the pharmacy that you weren't angry with me. But you still are, aren't you?''

''No, Conner,'' she told him. ''Please believe me. This isn't about you.''

He couldn't help but ask, ''Then…what is it about?''

Her beautiful face was filled with roiling emotion and he was certain there was more she wanted to say. Yet she didn't.

He found himself staring at her glorious golden hair when she dipped her chin toward her chest.

She murmured, ''It's almost over. Everything's set.'' Then her gaze skimmed the inn and she sighed heavily.

Now, Mattie thought, would be the perfect moment to tell Conner everything. To explain about her work. To tell him that she'd love to attend Lori and Grey's party with him, but that she'd spent some long hours on a plan to send Brenda and Scotty in secret to the southwest, where they would begin a new life for themselves.

But she looked up at Freedom Trail and knew Brenda was in there watching her. Mattie knew from her own experience how afraid Brenda was of her safe haven being discovered, even though she knew Mattie trusted Conner.

Every time Susan had gone into hiding, the fear of discovery that the entire family had dealt with had been devastating. Brenda was feeling that right now.

She'd promised Brenda she'd tell no one. And it was a promise she simply had to keep. At least until mother and son boarded that midnight bus bound for New Mexico.

"What do you mean when you say that everything is set?"

Conner's question forced her to meet his dark gaze. She injected a brightness into her words as she said, "What I mean is that tomorrow we can begin work on the carriage house. Everything is set and I'm ready. But right now—" she made a show of looking at her wristwatch "—you'll have to go. I've got an appointment in just ten minutes."

Joseph was coming to meet with Brenda. Mattie didn't want Conner to be here when his grandfather arrived.

Those onyx eyes of Conner's studied her in silence. It was clear he wasn't sure what to think.

Finally he nodded slowly. "If I don't see you at Grey's house tonight, I'll be here bright and early in the morning."

Mattie hated letting him walk away with all those doubts in his head about her, but she honestly felt that she had no choice.

Scotty set three plates on the table and then went to the cutlery drawer for forks, knives and spoons. He was sad, and the child wasn't even trying to hide it. Mattie stood at the stove, stirring the beef stew she was heating for their dinner.

Brenda was talking with Joseph in the privacy of the living room while Mattie and Scotty fixed the meal.

"I'm not going to see you again, am I?" the boy asked Mattie.

"I won't lie to you, sweetie. You probably won't."

Worry settled on the child's shoulders like a fuzzy gray cloud, but he continued at his task, folding the linen napkins into neat rectangles and then placing the utensils on top of them.

"Why does my dad have to be so mean? Why does he hurt my mom? I hate him so much. I never want to see him again."

Mattie covered the Dutch oven with its heavy lid and then turned her soft gaze onto Scotty.

"We have to go away, don't we?" he asked Mattie.

She nodded. "Your mom thinks it's for the best. So you'll both be safe."

Scotty nodded now, and Mattie's heart ached with

the knowledge that he was being forced to deal with things that children simply shouldn't have to deal with. But reality was reality, and it couldn't be avoided forever.

"I like you," he said. "And I like this place."

This was his way of telling her he appreciated everything she'd done, Mattie knew. She patted his shoulder and assured him, "I like you, too, Scotty. And the place you're going is just as nice. The people there will help you, just as I helped you. You and your mom are going to be all right."

The two of them shared a smile.

She looked up to see Joseph Thunder standing in the doorway.

To Scotty, Mattie said, "Why don't you go get washed up for dinner? Tell your mother we'll eat soon."

The boy hurried off.

"Thank you for coming," she said to Joseph. "Do you think Brenda is ready to go off on her own?"

"Do not worry," the old shaman said softly. "She will be fine. She has a very strong incentive for surviving. Her son."

That much was true, Mattie knew. Brenda showed the fierceness of a lioness when it came to protecting Scotty.

Joseph came toward her. "What I am more interested in talking about is you."

Surprised, Mattie said, "Me?"

He chuckled softly and took her hand in his. A calming vibration emanated from him.

"Yes, you. I feel that you have been spending much time feeling troubled."

Mattie's head bobbed up and down. "I've been worried sick about Brenda and—"

"No." Joseph stopped her. "I am speaking of the anxiety you are suffering over my grandson."

Hiding the fact that she was surprised by his perception was impossible. "Conner," she breathed.

How could Joseph know of her disquieting thoughts and feelings regarding Conner? But then, she shouldn't be the least astonished. The Kolheek people didn't let just anyone become a shaman. Joseph Thunder had been born with gifts and talents that bordered on the mystical.

He gazed deeply into her eyes, and Mattie got the sense that the elderly man was much older than he claimed to be. It was a silly notion, she knew. But in his dark eyes she sensed a mysterious insight, the wisdom of a thousand years.

"It is best," he said slowly, clearly, "that Conner blame me for the past."

Mattie gasped. "But you can't have done what he thinks. You need to talk to him. Tell him—"

"My child…"

This term of endearment made her go quiet, made her eyes well with emotion.

"Conner is not ready to see the truth. He may never be ready. You must understand that some things cannot be seen merely by opening the eyes. Sometimes it is a matter of opening the heart."

A chill coursed down the length of Mattie's spine. She desperately hated the idea that Conner's heart might be forever closed. That he would refuse to see the truth.

"Joseph," Mattie whispered around the knot that

had formed in her throat, "I know that you're a good man. I know you love Conner. I could see it in your eyes when we came to visit you." She paused long enough to swallow. "What is the truth? Did you take Conner away from his father?"

Sadness rose up and over the old shaman like an engulfing tidal wave.

"I did," he professed. "But it was all in my grandson's best interest. You see, my oldest son, Conner's father, was my namesake. Joe's wife died early in their marriage, when Conner was still a baby. Joe was never able to get over losing the love of his life. He drowned his grief in alcohol."

Although the story was terribly painful, Joseph's gaze never broke from hers.

"I tried everything to help my son," he continued. "I lectured. I forced him into rehabilitation more than once. But it was not to be. Joe was determined to go to the other side to be with Dee. I believe with all my heart that that was his intention. My greatest fear back then was that he would take Conner with him, for he had a habit of drinking and driving…often with my grandson in the car."

With sorrow thick in the air, he concluded, "I surrendered my son in order to save my grandson."

A tear of quiet distress slipped down Mattie's cheek. "You must tell him." Her voice was husky with emotion. "Conner is angry with you. And that anger is wrongly focused. You can make this right."

Joseph gave her fingers a gentle squeeze. "What is right is that Conner is happy. If he blames me, if he's angry with me, then he can continue to remember a father he adores."

Joseph *was* a good man. Mattie had known it all along. Her tears fell freely as she hugged him tight. She wished Conner could see Joseph for what he truly was.

Almost as if he discerned her thoughts, Joseph pulled away from her and warned, "It is not for us to change a person's destiny. Our job is only to help those we can. Just like Brenda in there. You did not choose this hard path she's about to take, but you are helping her in every way you can. It's a fine line we walk in this life, don't you think?"

Mattie swiped away a tear. "Sometimes, Joseph, it's a very fine line."

Conner was in a sour mood and a party was the last place he should be. And he knew his dark frame of mind was the result of the change in Mattie.

When the two of them had first met, she'd been open with her emotions. Yes, she'd been tearful that first night, fraught with distress. But after that, she'd been friendly, even flirtatious. They had enjoyed being together.

Then something had happened to change her behavior. And he didn't have any idea what it could be. Mattie had become a very secretive lady.

Yes, he'd boldly pointed out the powerful allure that seemed to pulse between them. Even told her that, until he figured out the mystery behind his nightmares and the feeling he had of not being whole, he didn't think he should be entertaining the potent thoughts and feelings he was experiencing toward her. However, he didn't think that was the cause of the change in her.

They had disagreed about the conclusions he'd come to regarding his grandfather. But that was okay. She was entitled to her opinion, and she couldn't know what he'd gone through as a child, the loneliness he'd suffered growing up without his father.

The sound of her voice drew him to the doorway, where he watched her greeting his cousin Grey and Grey's pregnant wife, Lori. He was surprised by the demonstrative manner in which Mattie was welcomed. Grey hugged her, then kissed her cheek, as did Lori. It was clear that these people were close. Very close.

Why, over the weeks, hadn't Mattie explained that she knew his family on such intimate terms? Conner found it odd.

He watched as Grey helped Mattie out of her light jacket.

Great Spirit above, she looked good. She wore a red cardigan sweater with a matching top underneath it. Her black skirt struck her midthigh, showing off a mile's worth of shapely leg. His gaze traveled down over her well-formed knees, tight calves, tiny ankles, to her feet that were swathed in black high-heeled pumps.

He'd never fancied himself a man who paid attention to fashion, but Mattie looked so good in that outfit, he began to salivate. His throat convulsed in a swallow.

Like radar, her clear blue eyes found him. She smiled, and every doubt that plagued him seemed to dissolve into thin air. As she made her way toward him, she greeted everyone she met. Still, that undercurrent of tension he sensed in her remained around her mouth and eyes. He just knew there was something going on that she was keeping to herself, something that was causing her a tremendous amount of stress. He wished he could say or do something that would ease the anxiety he saw in her face, relieve the strain she was under.

Remembering how she'd responded to his passionate touch in the past, he pondered pulling her to him and kissing the daylights out of her. That would startle every ounce of nervous tension from her body…and it would fill her with another kind of tension entirely.

The mere notion of doing such a thing had him grinning from ear to ear. He couldn't help it.

Mattie sidled up to him, "Is it warm in here, or is it me?"

"Oh, I'm pretty sure it's just you." He hoped his tone conveyed that he thought she looked quite hot, indeed. The kind of hot that had nothing whatsoever to do with air temperature.

Evidently she understood his meaning, because her cheeks flamed pink, enhancing her beauty further.

She unbuttoned her sweater and let it slide down her arms, then draped it over the back of a nearby chair. Conner couldn't help but notice how the red knit shell she wore underneath cuddled the curve of her rounded breasts.

"You want a glass of wine?" he offered. "Or a soda, mineral water, a beer?"

"A soda would be great. I can't drink alcohol this evening. I'm driving."

"You could have drunk like a fish," he quipped,

"if you'd come to the party with me rather than on your own."

She chuckled, but didn't respond. Conner went to the refreshment table to pour two glasses of soda.

From where he stood, he watched as another cousin, Nathan, approached Mattie. Nathan's fiancée was with him—Gwen, a fiery-haired beauty who was a schoolteacher. The three of them greeted one another like old friends, with hugs and kisses all around. It was clear that Nathan, Gwen and Mattie were more than casual acquaintances.

The three of them talked for a bit and then slipped out the door that led to the patio. Conner waited until the fizz in the sodas died down, and then he made his way across the room to where he'd been standing with Mattie.

Nathan, Gwen and Mattie were clearly embroiled in a serious discussion. Then Nathan did the strangest thing. He pulled out his wallet and gave Mattie several bills, which she slipped into her purse.

Something odd was going on. Something very odd.

At that moment Conner had the thought that Mattie was a great enigma so deep, so profound that figuring her out would take a man a lifetime of trying.

She would be worth every second of the endeavor.

As he went closer to the door, his hip brushed against the chair there and Mattie's red cardigan slipped to the floor. Conner set down both glasses of soda, bent and reached for the sweater. Without thinking, he lifted it to his face and inhaled Mattie's rain-fresh scent. His blood chugged sluggishly, thickly through his veins.

He paused, his gaze locked on the scarlet, finely knit fabric. As he crouched there beside the chair, his mind began to churn with troubling thoughts.

There had been a discernible difference in Mattie over the course of these past couple of weeks. The change in her, and the fact that he couldn't figure out the cause, was what had put him in such a gray mood. From what he could recollect, the change had occurred after the night they'd had dinner together at Freedom Trail.

Images raced through his head as he remembered the times they had spent together. Since the night she'd cooked that fabulous meal for him, since they'd shared that sizzling kiss on her deck at sunset, he realized he hadn't been back inside the inn.

The day he'd come to tell her about having used the herb his grandfather had given him, Mattie had suggested they take a walk. She'd led him away from her B and B even though she'd still been wearing her nightgown.

And she'd insisted on postponing work on the carriage house with the flimsy excuse that she wanted to wait for the building permit to arrive, even after he'd told her it was common practice in the construction business that, as long as she'd filed for the permit, the work could begin.

He found it more than a little odd that she knew his family so well. That she was friends with Grey's wife, with Nathan's fiancée, yet she had never felt the inclination to tell Conner this information. Facts that would seem quite ordinary and common to relate in everyday conversation.

And Mattie had defended his grandfather so fervently when Conner had angrily declared Joseph had separated him from his father. She'd have to know Joseph pretty well to endorse him so zealously, wouldn't she?

He thought about their meeting earlier today when he'd delivered the plans he'd drafted. Before Mattie had arrived, the hair on the back of his neck had risen and he'd had the definite feeling of being watched. Someone had been inside the inn. Someone other than an innocent guest who was visiting the New England mountains. This person had been hiding from him, or from someone. His intuition made him feel sure of it.

He'd already attempted the route of out-and-out asking her what was bothering her. More than once, in fact. But she'd remained mulishly vague.

Then there was the matter of the money Nathan had just given Mattie. That confused the hell out of him. Their conversation seemed so serious, the passing of the bills surreptitious.

He scrubbed at his chin. It was as if he had the pieces to a huge puzzle, but for the life of him, he couldn't seem to make them fit into any order…into any identifiable picture.

Curiosity was what made him fold Mattie's sweater up neatly and tuck it behind the chair, where it would be easily overlooked by everyone…but him.

He stood, picked up the sodas he'd poured and headed for the patio.

But that soft red sweater never left his mind. It

would afford him the opportunity to seek her out later. To find some answers to some immense and disconcerting questions that were stacking up like so many bricks in a wall.

For the next thirty minutes Conner and Mattie chatted with other guests, laughed at Nathan's stories of the antics of his six-year-old daughter and oohed and aahed over the gifts Lori had asked people not to bring, but graciously accepted when they were presented to her.

Conner couldn't help but notice how Mattie kept glancing at her watch. As they enjoyed a moment alone in one corner of the living room, he teasingly asked, "You have someplace you need to be?"

Her blue gaze didn't waver as she replied, "Actually, I do. And I should make my excuses to the hosts." She set her empty glass on the coffee table and made to stand up, but he stopped her by placing his fingers on her forearm.

"Wait, Mattie," he said. The moment his flesh contacted hers, it was as if someone had doused him in a flammable liquid and tossed a match at him. He was on fire for her. "I want to ask you something. Something important."

She relaxed into the chair, waiting.

"I know," he began haltingly, feeling unsure of what he wanted to say, "that I told you I wasn't interested in…well, in getting involved in a relationship until I'd found some answers. Until I found the reasons behind these dreams. But I believe I've made some discoveries. I think I—"

"Stop a minute, Conner," she said.

Discomfort fairly vibrated from her.

"I can't help but point out," she continued, "that we disagreed big time about the so-called discoveries you made."

He'd been about to explore the possibility that they might have a chance together. But here she was wanting to argue.

The obstinate expression on her features told him she meant to have her say, yet at the same time she seemed to be choosing her words carefully.

"If your grandfather really is the horrible person you think him to be," she said, "why are you still at Smoke Valley? Why haven't you told him exactly what you think of him and gone back to Boston where you've been all these years?"

Before he could even think of an answer to her startling questions, she ever-so-softly plowed ahead. "I think it's because you really aren't certain about those so-called discoveries."

She looked down at where his fingers still rested on her arm, and when her gaze rose to his, her eyes were clouded with what he perceived to be a poignant sadness.

"I really do have to go, Conner." She stood up then. "I need to go say goodbye to Lori and Grey, but if you'll walk me out to my car, it will give me a chance to tell you something. Something that…I hope…will help you to understand me just a little more."

Conner followed her to where his cousin and wife were standing in the kitchen. Mattie kissed them both and apologized for leaving so early.

In a normal situation, Conner would have expected the hosts of any party to attempt to coerce a guest not to leave early. But that wasn't how Grey and Lori acted at all. They accepted Mattie's regret, and wished her well, their tones holding what Conner could only describe as a grave quality.

Odd to the point of being peculiar, Conner thought.

He got the distinct impression that they were all privy to some secret that they were intent on keeping to themselves.

Whatever this mysterious matter was would be reaching some climax tonight. A turning point was about to be made. Conner knew that, because Mattie had invited him to begin work on the renovation project tomorrow.

As he helped Mattie into her jacket, he thought of the red sweater. The honorable thing for him to do was to remind her she'd left it in the living room, fetch it for her before she left.

But he didn't do either. That sweater was his only chance to discover what she was involved in.

He was prepared to get a little reckless in order to uncover Mattie's secret.

Chapter Eight

Guilt hounded Mattie as she made her way to her car. Conner was so close she could feel the heat of him, could inhale the woodsy scent of his cologne.

She was lying to him by omission, keeping from him the truth about herself, about her work, and that made her feel ashamed.

Tomorrow will come, a tiny voice piped up optimistically. *Brenda and Scotty will be safely on their way to Albuquerque. The term of your pledge to remain silent will be over. You can confess everything to Conner. You can lay your soul bare.*

Tomorrow.

Until then, Mattie realized, there was something she could offer him. Something that was terribly important to her.

Mattie looked up at the inky velvet of the night sky, let her eyes rove over the thousand points of glittering lights as she gathered together the inner strength it was going to take to tell the story of her past without getting upset. Tears were the last thing she needed tonight.

"When we first met," she began slowly, "you asked me about Susan. About my sister." She stopped, turned to face Conner, resting her rear on the driver-side door of her car. "I know you realized that I...well, I changed the subject back then." Her chagrin was expressed in a light chuckle. "And not very fluidly, either."

The sigh she emitted came from deep inside. "It's difficult for me to talk about Susan. What happened to her had a huge impact on me. On everyone who loved her."

Evidently sensing her trepidation, Conner reached out to her, smoothed his palm down along her arm. "If it upsets you," he told her, "then you don't have to talk about it, Mattie."

"But I do. I want you to better understand me. Who I am. What I stand for. Why I do the things I do. Where my life is destined to go."

Seeming to grasp the enormity of what she was about to explain, he let his hand fall to his side, then balled his fists and slipped them into the pockets of his black trousers.

Lord, but he looked good in that deep green crew-necked cable knit, the collar of his black dress shirt folded neat and tidy at the base of his neck. The sweater emphasized his strong chest, made her want to rest her head there, take the comfort she remembered he'd given so willingly by the lake that first night.

"Susan was my older sister," she said. "By five

years. I looked up to her as we grew up." Despite
the terrible ending that she knew was coming, Mattie
couldn't help but smile as she thought of her childhood here in these Vermont mountains. "My parents
were busy making a go of the B and B, and Susan
and I were pretty free to roam around wherever we
pleased.

"I was devastated when she went off to college.
Boston seemed so very far away. And when she
came home to visit, she was changed. She didn't
have time to hike to the lake. She was too full of
stories of parties and boys."

Mattie braced herself, for now was the point where
she had to introduce the man whom she was still
striving hard not to hate.

"Jim was the captain of the football team," she
continued, relieved that her brother-in-law's name
rolled off her tongue with nary a hitch. "He was
attending college on a full scholarship. He was smart.
And funny. And Susan fell for him so hard that she
couldn't say which way was up."

The breeze was cool against Mattie's cheeks, but
she was oblivious to it. "Jim's family was from up
north, in Burlington. His father had a successful business taking fishermen on trips around Lake Cham-
plain and up into Canada. It seemed natural when
Susan and Jim married that they settle in Burlington,
where Jim worked with his father."

The breath she dragged into her lungs was shaky.
This was where the story became hairy.

"The first time Susan came home with
bruises—"

The horror of the memories silenced her. Her gaze

slid from Conner's and she pressed her fingers to her mouth. The silence of the New England night sounded deafening.

Keeping her eyes averted, letting her fingers drop an inch to curl at her chin, she forced herself to continue.

"Jim had beat her something awful," Mattie whispered. "She had cuts and abrasions all over her body. But the worst part about it was, she told us…Mom, Dad and me…th-that that hadn't been the first time it had happened."

She felt the need for support and wrapped her arms tight about herself. Mattie was seeing it in her head, as if the whole awful ordeal were happening all over again. Hearing her sister's tears, her parents' fear. Feeling her own inadequacy to help Susan.

"The thing that amazed me," she said, "was that Susan went back to him. She forgave that bastard and went home to Burlington. To Jim." Mattie lifted her chin, found Conner's dark gaze, focused on it. "Many times."

A needle of pain made her realize she was pinching her bottom lip between her teeth. She released it, and immediately her chin began to tremble.

"He killed her, Conner." Her voice was as ragged as a torn paper. "Jim murdered Susan. He pushed her and she struck her head. And there was nothing we could do to keep that tragedy from happening."

Conner's coal-black eyes shone with deep emotion. To think that he felt her sorrow, that he commiserated with her, was very consoling to her. Then she was enveloped in his strong arms, his hands sliding along her back.

"Oh, Mattie," he crooned. "My Mattie. May the Great Spirit above comfort you."

She reveled in the blessing, resting her cheek against his corded shoulder. Closing her eyes, she drank in the scent of him. Absorbed his heat. Basked in the respite he offered.

"It must have been a nightmare for you," he said, his breath soft against her ear. "For your parents, too."

She nodded, the back of her head grazing his chin.

Mattie was content to recount the rest of her story from this position, curled against the safety of his shoulder, his arms tight about her.

"Dad and Mom just couldn't take living here anymore," she told him. "So they retired to Florida and left me to run Freedom Trail. They're doing well, doing what they can to heal." A tear slipped from the corner of her eye. "But they'll never forget. They can't. None of us will ever forget."

"Honey…" Conner pulled her back, urged her to lift her head. His fingers caressed her jaw as he looked deep into her eyes. "You're not meant to forget something like that. Doing so would be impossible."

In a moment of weakness Mattie found herself admitting, "Th-there are times that I wish I *could* forget. I wish I could take that memory and rip it out of my brain. It hurts so bad to know that my sister was in pain, that she was in grave danger, and there wasn't a thing I could do about it."

There was understanding in his silence, in the softness of the depths of his eyes. Time seemed to slow. Mattie studied his handsome face and realized she was experiencing a small bit of tranquillity, something that had become a rarity in her life.

"The night we first met," she told him, her voice stronger now, "was the anniversary of Susan's death. I was feeling so sad." She smiled. "But…you helped me that night, Conner. Helped me to get through it. And for that I want to thank you."

His wide, sensuous mouth pulled into a smile. "If I helped you, then I'm pleased." After a moment he asked, "What happened to him? Your sister's husband, I mean."

"Jim's in prison. He'll be locked away for the rest of his life. Not every abuser-turned-murderer gets that long a sentence, especially if their crime isn't seen as premeditated. But we were lucky. We got full justice for Susan."

Conner slid the pad of his fingers into the hollow of her cheek, stroked the sensitive underside of her jaw with his thumb. Mattie got the impression that he knew they were going to break apart soon, and he was savoring every moment of being near her. Her heart warmed.

Smoothing her splayed palms down his chest, she used them as leverage to ease herself away from him. "I really do need to go now. But thank you for listening. I…well, I wanted you to understand."

"Understand?"

The bewilderment he felt was evident in the way his arched brows drew together.

She bobbed her head in two quick jerks. "Me." That was all she could afford to say at the moment.

Tomorrow. She sent out the silent, whispery promise. Tomorrow she would be free to reveal all.

His expression brightened with the emergence of what he must have thought was an answer to his own question.

"You're explaining why you're still single," he said. He took a backward step, his head nodding with what looked to be solemn satisfaction. He almost seemed proud to have figured her out. "Why you're…unattached."

His conclusion was only partly correct. The whole of the matter was that she'd felt guilty for not telling him about her work. She'd meant to offer him a little…something. Something that would help him to understand her. Something that would help him to appreciate the rest of what she intended to relay tomorrow morning.

The idea obviously disturbed him. "Mattie, you're not allowing what happened to your sister to—"

His lips pressed together, and she knew he was having difficulty finding the words he wanted to say. He looked off down the street, then swung his gaze back to her face.

"If you cut yourself off from living," he said gently, "you're condemning yourself to the same kind of life sentence as Susan's murderer."

Scalding tears squeezed painfully from Mattie's eyes as shock froze every muscle in her body. Never had she expected Conner to put her on the same plane as her brother-in-law.

Before this moment, Mattie had always believed she shied away from relationships, away from men, because her work with abused women necessitated a strict secrecy. A complete and utter confidentiality.

And it was her commitment to those things that allowed the women she aided to trust her.

Women just like Brenda.

But Conner had boiled it down into something awful, likening her solitary lifestyle to being imprisoned. Locked away. Like Jim.

She pushed herself away from her car, defensiveness striking a spark of hot ire in her.

"I'm not stupid," she said. "I don't believe that every man I meet is capable of the kind of violence Susan experienced with Jim."

The force of her anger had him backing away. "Hold on. I wasn't suggesting that there's anything wrong with your intelligence, Mattie."

She yanked open the door of her car.

"Wait." Conner looked stunned as he spoke—she saw his stark reflection in the window. "I never said—"

She whirled to face him. "I haven't always lived like a nun, you know," she blurted, the silly justification making her want to cringe. "I've dated. Plenty of times, buster. But some things are more important than…than…*men.*"

Why on earth had she become so antagonistic with Conner? Had she really snipped that she hadn't lived like a nun? Had she actually called him *buster?*

She had. A groan broke the silence in the car as she turned into her driveway.

Well, he'd stunned her. Completely.

Mattie had always thought of her isolated life as something that was honorable. She kept herself secluded because secrecy was a big part of her work with the abused. These women were forced to go into hiding…forced to go underground for safety reasons.

In her mind, her lifestyle was necessary. Admirable, even.

However, when Conner had accused her of imprisoning herself, just as her murdering brother-in-law was imprisoned, Mattie had felt as if she'd been slapped in the face.

She cut the engine, but remained seated in the car. Her fingers smoothed along the curve of the steering wheel, resting at the base of the cool, knobby circle.

Could Conner be right? Was it possible that she'd sentenced herself to a life of loneliness? That her sister's death had caused her to open her compassion to hurting women, but close her heart to love?

Unwittingly she pressed her fingertips to her mouth, the memory of Conner's kiss strong and concentrated enough to cause her heart to quicken, even though she was sitting all alone in the darkness.

Mattie seemed to remember that each time she and Conner would get close, each time the attraction between them tugged and pulled at her like some invisible rope, she'd make an excuse about why she couldn't surrender to the delicious feelings that throbbed through her body when he looked at her. When he touched her.

Reaching for her purse on the seat beside her, she shoved open the door and got out of the car. She'd spent five years dedicating herself to this cause. Was she going to let one man make her question what she was doing, or how and why she was doing it?

The uneven ground was difficult to cross in her high heels. Clumps of grass snagged her steps.

She'd been terribly careful when she'd talked with Conner at the party. At one point he'd tried to convince her that he'd found the reason behind his nightmare, but she'd had to disagree with him. Again.

Just as Joseph had expressed, she'd walked the fine line. What she'd wanted to do was tell Conner everything she knew. Make him see, once and for all, that his grandfather wasn't the enemy Conner thought, but a loving advocate who was willing to shoulder the blame for the past if that would help Conner to preserve good memories of his father.

However, Joseph had told her Conner wasn't ready for the truth. That he might not ever be ready. Mattie felt it wasn't her place to force something on him for which he was unprepared.

She slipped the key into the lock and pushed open the front door.

''Brenda?'' she called. It would be time to go soon. She had to put aside these personal matters and focus on the here and now.

For the next several hours, getting Brenda and her son out of town safely would be her only goal, her only thought.

Brenda came down the stairs. Mattie marveled at the determination she witnessed on the woman's face. Anxiety was there, too, but resolve firmed her jaw. It hadn't been very long ago that Brenda's moral fiber had been weak as a wet paper sack. Mattie had doubted the woman's ability to make it on her own.

But once again Mattie realized the elderly shaman had made a declaration that had been dead-on when he'd said that Scotty would be the reason Brenda survived. It was amazing how maternal instincts took over when a fearful woman had children to protect.

"Are you and Scotty packed? It's nearly time to go."

The woman nodded. "Scotty's watching TV upstairs. I perked us a pot of coffee. It's waiting in the kitchen. I thought we could sit and have a cup before we go." Shyly she said, "I've got some things I want to say to you, Mattie."

Over cups of steaming coffee Brenda expressed her heartfelt appreciation.

"I don't know what I'd have done if you hadn't been there for me and Scotty," she told Mattie. "You took us in. Gave us a place to stay for free. Fed us. You bought us clothes. Even suitcases." Tears glistened in the woman's eyes as she said, "And you talked to me. Made me see that there are people who care about me. People who want to see me happy." Her voice hitched as she added, "People who want to see me free."

Her inhalation was shaky, but she continued. "I've never met anyone as giving as you, Mattie. Never."

Setting her cup on the table, Mattie leaned toward Brenda, reaching out to her with the intent of graciously accepting the woman's thanks. But a shadow fell across the kitchen floor.

Although Brenda attempted to stifle herself, her high-pitched squeal made Mattie flinch, the hair on her scalp rising with the adrenaline that flooded her system. Porcelain shattered on the floor. Coffee sloshed across the oak floorboards.

Mattie's mind raced with a plan to save Brenda, Scotty and herself from an enraged Tommie Boy.

She scrambled to put herself between Brenda and the doorway, her gaze finally rising...to see Conner's astounded face staring back at her.

"What's going on here?" he asked, his brow marred with a sharp frowning crease as he took in every aspect: the unmitigated panic that hung in the air, the yellowish bruises on Brenda's battered face, the broken coffee cup, Mattie's fumbling but clearly protective maneuvering.

Time itself seemed to shift into low gear. Mattie felt her chest heave as she gulped in air. Relief knowing they weren't in any actual danger made her weak in the knees, but anger ignited in her like a flash fire in dry forest.

"What are you doing, Conner?" she demanded. "You can't just barge in here—"

"I knocked. And the door was open."

Heavens, how stupid could she be? Leaving the door open for anyone to just waltz right into her home?

Conner held up her sweater. "You left this at Grey and Lori's." He set it on the counter, then turned his dark gaze on her again.

"I didn't hear your truck pull up." The accusation in her tone was unmistakable. What was wrong with her? Why was she attacking him? For the life of her, she couldn't say.

"I jogged over from the cabin," he told her. "It's a clear night." His gaze darted to Brenda and then back to Mattie. "So...you want to tell me what's going on?"

Realizing that his motives were innocent, that he'd

arrived only to bring back her sweater should have calmed the turmoil in her mind. But it didn't. The fury that licked at her like scorching flames was out of control, fueled by surplus adrenaline and leftover fear. All she knew was that the inferno blazed, turning rational thought to ashes.

"No," she said, unable to contain the volume of her voice. "I'm not going to tell you anything, Conner. This is none of your business."

Silence throbbed in the air like a living, breathing thing.

Surprisingly, it was Brenda who broke it. "Mattie's helping me," she said, her voice soft but purposeful. "My husband…h-he ain't no good. I'm catching a bus tonight. Mattie paid for my ticket."

Conner's midnight eyes never left Mattie's face, the expression reflected in them unreadable. A moment passed. Then another. She felt as if her larynx had become paralyzed. Without another word he turned on his heel and disappeared from sight.

The sound of the front door closing made Mattie start.

"Oh, Mattie," Brenda said. "He's angry. You need to go after him. Explain things to him. Make him understand." She pointed toward the window. "There he goes. He's heading toward the woods."

Irritation had Mattie snapping, "You don't go running after a man just because he's angry, Brenda. All that does is get you into deeper trouble. I've been lecturing on that from the first day you came here."

Brenda's spine straightened with resentfulness. "With my husband, maybe," she said. "But he's not like Tommie Boy. You know it, and so do I. All he's done is come around trying to help you out, Mattie. And you kept shooin' him away all on account o' me.''

The haze in her head began to clear. Mattie swallowed. ''I was going to tell him everything once you were safely on your way. Tomorrow.'' Mattie's gaze turned to the window and she watched Conner stalking across the lawn.

''Well, go change into your sneakers,'' Brenda urged. ''That man deserves an explanation.''

Unbeknownst to the women below in the kitchen, Conner's departure was being watched by someone else, too. A frightened little boy who was staring out an upstairs window.

Chapter Nine

Pushing his way into Mattie's home, into Mattie's personal business, had been a terrible mistake. Conner recognized that now. He shoved aside the pine bough that dipped into the path through the woods as he made his way back to the cabin. He should have left well enough alone. Even though he'd sensed Mattie had been hiding something, he knew her to be an honest, upright person. He should have realized that whatever her secret was, it couldn't be anything nefarious. But experiencing the brunt of her covert behavior and not knowing what it was all about had nearly driven him crazy.

No. Not crazy. It had driven him to do something he wouldn't normally have done. Hiding her sweater like that had been deceitful. Hell, he'd practically stolen it just so he'd have a reason to go snooping around. He frowned, realizing no good was ever gained by underhanded actions. He should be filled with guilt and remorse. He'd frightened Mattie and that woman who was staying with her half to death when he'd walked in on the two of them.

It would never have entered his head that Mattie might be involved in aiding the abused. However, the scenario made perfect sense after what she'd watched her sister go through, after experiencing an agonizing helplessness…not knowing what to do or where to go for support. Imagining the grief Mattie must have suffered after Susan's murder was next to impossible for Conner.

Seeing that battered woman standing in the kitchen of Freedom Trail had been the final piece to the puzzle…the essential element that had enabled him to put together the picture that was Mattie Russell.

He sighed as he entered a spot where the trail widened, the glassy surface of Smoke Lake becoming visible through the thinning scrub. Yes, he should be feeling terribly guilty about having encroached on Mattie's private affairs.

So why was he experiencing the sensation of having been stung? Slapped? Wounded? Conner was hurt by Mattie's secretiveness and by the harsh words she'd hurled at him a few moments ago.

Instinct as ancient as time itself had him going completely still, head angled, every sense on full alert. Faint footsteps fell on the loamy ground not too far behind him. The swoosh of fabric against the snagging limbs of a bush. Someone followed him.

The glow of moonlight on golden hair told him it was Mattie. Her steps slowed.

"Conner?"

The uncertainty in her tone tore at his heart. She hadn't yet seen him on the path.

"I'm here," he called.

She followed the sound of his voice to the lake-shore. The distress she felt was expressed on her delicate features, in her rounded shoulders, in the way her hands clenched into fists, then relaxed only to tighten up once again. About three feet from him, she stopped.

"All I can offer you is an apology." Her soft tone held a strong petitioning quality. "I wanted to tell you, Conner. I wanted to tell you everything. But I promised Brenda that I wouldn't. She was so scared, you see."

The words gushed from her.

"Her husband is a violent man. And when she first arrived, she trusted no one. Not even me. Her husband is hunting for her. He had flyers posted in Mountview. He's a dangerous man, Conner. You saw her face. I had to agree to Brenda's terms. Assuring her that she could trust me was all-important. I had to create a bond between us. Otherwise she might have gone back to him." Her voice fell to a rusty whisper as she added. "So many of them do."

The milky skin between her brows creased. "Please, Conner, try to understand. I had to keep this a secret."

He wanted to empathize with her. He wanted to understand. He did, actually. But suddenly it seemed that his wounded feelings began to ooze fresh blood.

"After seeing you with Grey and Lori, with Nathan and Gwen—" the enormity of the affront and hurt in his tone took him aback "—it seems that the only person you kept your secret from was me. And there seemed to be an amazing familiarity between you and my grandfather. Does he know, too?''

Her luscious mouth pursed as she nodded her head. ''He does,'' she admitted.

It was as if she'd reached out with her fingernails and torn fresh gashes in his flesh. His bark of laughter was grim. ''So why all the secrecy, Mattie? You make lame excuses to keep me away from the inn. Away from the carriage house. Away from *you*. Yet everyone knows what's going on there! Everyone but me.''

''Everyone doesn't know, Conner.''

His jaw dropped incredulously. ''I heard them. Grey and Lori were too eager to accept your non-existent explanation to leave the party early. And Gwen was standing right there when Nathan slipped you some money. My cousin is funding your cause. Are you going to deny that?''

''No, I'm not. I can't.''

The confession he'd wrung out of her should have made him feel vindicated, but it didn't. What she was doing was noble. So why was he feeling so angry? He had no answer as the cloud hovering over him only got thicker. Darker.

''They know about my work, yes,'' she said. ''Nathan has offered his help in case I need him. And Lori and Gwen…well, they came to me seeking help. They came to Vermont because they were both fleeing abusive relationships. Lori was being stalked by her ex-husband. And Gwen was trying to save her brother from a violent stepfather.''

Her chin tipped up determinedly. ''Like I said,

they know about my work. They're good friends, one
and all. They help when they can. They ask no questions. They don't discuss my work with anyone.
Ever. They don't know about specific individuals...when they arrive...or when they leave. Grey
treated Brenda's physical injuries. Joseph counseled
her. No one knows of her presence at Freedom Trail
except for Joseph and Grey." Quietly she added,
"And you."

Mattie's chest rose and fell several times. "You
probably won't believe this now, but...I was going
to tell you everything, Conner. Tomorrow morning.
Just as soon as Brenda was on her way."

She reached out to him then. Let her tapered fingers slide over his biceps.

His brain churned and boiled, and he drew in a
shaky breath. He wanted to believe her. He wanted—

A twig snapped and both their heads swiveled,
their gazes leveled on the shadowy trail from which
they both had come.

The boy was young, Conner saw. Not much more
than nine or ten.

"Scotty," Mattie said, surprise coating her tone,
"what are you doing out here in the dark? Honey,
does your mother know where you are?"

The child shook his head. "She'll be mad when
she finds out I left the house. But I was w-worried
about you, Mattie. I want you to come back now.
Okay?"

Distress filled the boy's gaze as it darted from
Mattie's face to Conner's and then back again. He
looked to Conner as if he wanted to bolt.

"You don't want us to miss our bus, Mattie,"

Scotty said. "We should go back now. We should be leaving for town soon."

Like the corroded cogs of some age-old machinery, Conner's brain finally ka-chunked with a grand, mind-blowing realization. Insight made him gasp.

"You're taking that boy from his father!" He leveled the accusation on Mattie as if he was indicting her for a crime. In his mind, what she was about to do *was* a crime.

"I want to go, Mattie."

The fear and pleading in the child's tone filtered into Conner's hazy mind, but he was too inundated with cataclysmic emotion to react properly to what he heard.

Conner couldn't take his eyes off Mattie's face. "Do you know what you're doing? Do you have any idea what it's like for a kid to grow up without his father? A boy *needs* his dad, Mattie."

His supplication was on Scotty's behalf. Conner knew what the child's life was going to be like. The empty ache that lasted for years…that never went away. But he had to admit that it was the still-grieving child deep inside him who cried out with such pain. Moisture scalded the backs of his eyelids, shattering his vision into sharp splinters illuminated by murky moonlight.

"I can't let you do it," he said. "I can't be a party to—"

"Conner."

The sheer determination in her tone sliced into his sentence like a well-honed blade of steel.

"I'm taking Brenda and Scotty to the bus station," she said, her voice dead calm. "And nothing you can say will stop me. If there was any other way to save them, don't you think I'd make it happen?''

Scotty came to stand beside Mattie. ''I want to go, Mattie. Please.''

Conner's shoulders rounded as he realized that the child was trembling, his eyes wide with anxiety. Crouching onto his haunches, Conner looked into the boy's face. ''You don't understand what's happening here. What's your last name, Scotty? Let me help you.''

''It's you who doesn't understand, Conner. This boy has witnessed things no child should ever see.'' Ire flashed in Mattie's sapphire eyes. ''He doesn't need you—no matter how good your intentions might be—to send him back to a place he doesn't want to be. To the kind of person his father is. He doesn't need the kind of help you're offering.''

Conner stood then, lifting his gaze to hers, ready for this face-off. ''I'm glad that I finally discovered the truth about you before...''

Before I completely lost my heart to you, was what he'd been about to utter. Thank the Great Spirit above, he'd been able to stop himself. Nothing made a man weaker than revealing his innermost thoughts to his adversary. And right at this moment that's how he viewed Mattie. As someone with whom he was in direct opposition.

Some unreadable emotion flickered in her gaze then, the anger that tensed her face easing.

''Conner, listen to me,'' she said. ''Please listen.'' She paused long enough to swallow, to moisten her full bottom lip. Her tone impassioned, she added, ''Some men don't deserve to be fathers.''

Then without another word she took the boy's hand and led him down the darkened trail.

Conner hacked at the sapling's base with the ax and felled the small tree in a single swing. He picked it up, stripped it of its limbs and then stacked it on the pile.

He had never realized that the human mind was capable of going through such changes as his was doing tonight. He would reach one conclusion only to find that that line of reckoning was erroneous, then another revelation would slam into his head with what seemed the speed of light.

The one and only issue he'd come to any firm verdict on was Mattie and his feelings for her.

He loved her. Of that he was certain, and he was man enough to admit that there would be no wavering on *that* observation.

It was due to the depth of his emotion for her that he'd made so many mistakes tonight. He'd forced his way into her private business. Then he'd had the audacity to feel hurt when she'd declared that what she was involved in was none of his concern. And when she'd tracked him down on the pathway through the forest to apologize, he'd actually accused her of letting everyone in the world in on her secret—everyone, that was, but him.

Mattie twisted his emotions inside out. He wanted her. She was a beautiful woman. But what he felt ran deeper than mere physical desire.

He admired her. Admired her courage for all she'd gone through, for her dedication to helping others.

Conner still wasn't convinced that separating that

boy from his father was the right thing for Mattie to be doing.

This boy has witnessed things no child should ever see. Her words rang through his head.

It had been wrong of him to make judgments against Mattie and her actions regarding the boy without knowing all the facts. She was an intelligent woman. She wouldn't be putting so much effort into dividing this family without good, solid reasons.

If there was any other way to save them...

Mattie's incensed appeal reverberated through his thoughts, reminding him of some other time...some other place. But he shoved the dark memories aside. He wasn't ready yet.

Wrapping his arms around the pile of saplings he'd cut, Conner dragged them to the clearing he'd made earlier. He stuck one flexible sapling in each of the narrow, shallow holes he'd dug, then he began to bend the trunks and secure them together with strips of bark. He stopped only to lay more wood on the fire he'd built to heat the rocks that would fill the sweat lodge with steam.

As he worked, the image of the little boy's eyes haunted him. The boy's fear had been immense, that much had been obvious. It bothered Conner to know that *he* had been the object of Scotty's terror.

The child had stirred something in Conner's subconscious, or rather the boy's angst had. Again Conner shoved away the dark clouds that threatened. He wanted to complete the lodge before he opened the door to the past.

Once more, Mattie's voice whispered through his head, *Some men don't deserve to be fathers.*

Like a double-edged sword, her words had held dual meaning. She'd intended to push home the idea that Scotty would be better off without his violent father…and Conner suspected she'd been offering another message, as well. One that at first had offended him to no end. Had she insinuated that his father had been in some way unworthy?

In that instant he'd felt as if he'd been standing before her already wounded and bleeding, yet she'd coldly delivered the fatal blow.

He'd come back to the cabin to pace its close confines, too angry with Mattie to even think straight. But over time his ire had subsided enough that common sense had filtered into the chaos rioting in his mind. Rather than having a calming effect, though, logic only had him agitated all over again.

Not with anger—no, his anger was spent, gone. But he was suddenly captured by a single-minded determination to solve the mystery of his dreams— of his past—once and for all.

With the frame of the sweat lodge complete, Conner went in search of several thick boughs from a pine tree that would contain the steam and heat. As he secured the fragrant pine to the sapling framework, he sent out a silent prayer of appreciation to Mother Earth for supplying his needs this night.

Conner smothered the fire and then used a heavy Y-shaped stick to transfer the pile of hot rocks from the smoldering embers to the sweat lodge. Then he picked up the bucket of water he'd hauled from the lake. Tugging his sweatshirt from his body, he secured it over the opening in the lodge. He crouched down and crawled into the cramped confines of the lodge he'd built.

Thoughts of Mattie floated in and out of his mind, but he did what he could to ignore them. There was so much that needed working out, so many dilemmas to solve. But right now he had to focus on himself.

It was time to face the memories—*the realities*—of his childhood.

Conner cleared his mind of all anxiety. The water he ladled from the bucket sizzled as it came into contact with the rocks. Closing his eyes, he inhaled, pulling the scent of pine and hot steam deep into his lungs. He fixed his thoughts, his inner sight, on a tiny pinprick of light that he conjured in his mind. His spiritual ear heard the sounds of ancient Kolheek meditating drums that beat to the simultaneous rhythm of his heart.

With his breathing slow and steady, his thoughts void, Conner let himself slip into a dreamy state of consciousness.

The blackness behind his eyelids lightened and a smoky haze seemed to billow as images gradually emerged. Just as in his familiar nightmare, the first sensation he became aware of was the heat.

Next, the shapes took form: the frightening, animated bear, the mighty oak. And yet again Conner found himself separated from the happenings in the dream by a thin veil of pure white light. The glowing curtain gave off the feeling of security, protectiveness, a shroud through which Conner could see the dream, but not be affected by it. Prior to returning to the rez, the dreams had been so harrowing that he would awaken with his heart in his throat, a sheen of sweat on his body.

Then he realized that even after returning to Smoke Valley, he had been jarred awake, panting and fearful. So when exactly had this shielding cloak become an element of his dream?

Conner remembered that the last time he'd experienced the dream as a full-fledged nightmare had been in Mattie's home. He'd awakened with a start from where he'd fallen asleep on her couch. After that incident, the dream had ceased to be so nightmarish and had become more of a night vision that needed sorting through. A problematic apparition that required deciphering.

He had no idea how or why Mattie might have caused this change, but he was grateful for it nonetheless.

Sinking deeper into the mental picture from the past, Conner realized that the small boy from his dream—he, himself—was standing outside his grandfather's sweat lodge, his face pressed against the soft pine as he peered through the cracks between the saplings. Never before had the images been so clear.

No wonder the heat in his nightmare had been so intense. He watched as his grandfather ladled water onto the huge pile of rocks. The air wafting about his face was sweltering, but what was taking place inside the lodge was too important for him to back away.

An odd feeling of disembodiment gave Conner the sensation of being the anxious and guilt-ridden little boy while standing on the sidelines behind the screen of light, calmly watching the proceedings take place.

Apprehension urged him to lift himself out of the image, to wipe the dream—no, the memory—from his mind and not deal with it. But doing so was no longer a possibility. The truth had to be faced. As a young Kolheek he was taught that truth could never harm. It might be a teacher of hard lessons, but one was better off walking in the wisdom of reality than stumbling in the darkness of idealism.

Wrapping himself in the light, he pressed to become one with the boy. He needed to see through the child's eyes.

Inside the sweat lodge an argument was taking place. His father was there. And his grandfather, too. The two men were locked in a battle of wills.

He was startled to see that the image he had always taken to be the animated bear, swinging out its sharp-clawed paws, did not have the face of his grandfather. The bear was his father. Furious, shouting, insistent…and staggering drunk.

"You cannot take Conner from me," he bellowed. "He is my son! You are an old fool if you think you can steal my boy."

Unrelenting, Joseph Thunder stood as firm as a mighty oak.

"You will leave Smoke Valley," he said to his son. "And you will not return until you have stopped drinking. Conner will stay with me. I will get the elders involved if I have to."

Involving the tribal elders in a family dispute was the equivalent of going to federal court—the consequences were that binding.

Gut-wrenching guilt lay heavy in the belly of the eavesdropping boy, and the reasoning behind that fearful remorse came flooding into Conner's brain with the speed of a rushing, rain-swollen river.

Conner remembered having gone to his grandfather. Remembered having complained about his fear of riding in the car with his father. Remembered describing the way the car would swerve from one side of the road to the other.

His grandfather had hugged him tightly and told him not to worry, that he would take care of everything.

And he had.

Joseph Thunder had banished his son from the rez. He had taken custody of Conner. Had raised him as his own.

And how had Conner repaid the man? By conveniently forgetting that he himself was the impetus behind the drastic change in his life. As a six-year-old boy, he had "tattled" on his father, thus resulting in the exile that had left him aching and lonely for the very man whom he'd betrayed. Conner realized it was that little boy's guilt that had caused him to forget. He'd put the truth out of his mind in order to live with the fact that *he* had been the cause of his father's going away.

Memories continued to rain down in a torrent.

His father had worked as a deliveryman, driving long distances to and from towns all over New England. And it was common practice that Conner would accompany his father. It was these very trips that Conner had complained to his grandfather about…and it was on one of these trips not three months after being exiled from the rez that Joe Thunder had died.

A scalding tear welled from Conner's closed eyes, trailing down his face as he remembered that his father hadn't been killed *by* a drunk driver, but *had been* the drunk driver who had caused the accident that had taken his life.

The fancies of a child who wanted a perfect parent had caused him to twist and turn the truth into a dark ideal. And he'd spent quite a few years stumbling around in it, too.

Conner wept. He mourned the death of his father. He also grieved for all the years he'd lost with his grandfather. He'd wasted so much time—too much time—blaming the man who loved him, who had saved him.

There was nothing he could do that would bring his father back, he realized. But although he couldn't bring back a single day of those years spent impugning his grandfather, he could still make things right with his grandfather. Starting today.

Hope budded in his chest like a flower, fragrant and beautiful.

The images in his head had evaporated like morning mist. But Conner sat there, still and silent, realizing that the glowing veil remained. It radiated with a peculiar and mysterious light. A light that was nearly lifelike.

The curtain drew in upon itself, gathered up into a ball and metamorphosed into a pristine-white dove. Its wings fluttered gracefully. Its coo brought peace to his mind, tranquillity to his soul.

He placed all his concentration on the lovely bird…and it transformed yet again.

The bird's eyes turned a familiar sapphire-blue, its downy face became Mattie's milky complexion, her beautiful features smiling, and the snowy wings flowed into her long, wind-whipped hair. Conner drew in an awestruck breath.

Then the image was gone.

Many ancient Kolheek legends surrounded love. Tradition told of how one's life partner would arrive in a dream as a totem, a special and revered symbol that would shapeshift into the face of the beloved.

Conner sat in the lodge, his body relaxed, his mind at ease, and he realized that Mattie had come as a dove because peace was what he'd needed most. Although she hadn't forced him to face his fears, she had encouraged him in every way possible to confront his dream, to discover the truth behind it.

He'd learned so many things tonight. About himself, his father, his grandfather, his past. But he smiled at the greatest revelation of all, the knowledge that surpassed all else, the wisdom that set his heart and mind free…

Mattie was his soul mate.

Chapter Ten

As Conner parked his truck outside his grandfather's house, the sun was just cresting the vandyked mountaintop. Streaks of prismatic pink swathed the crystalline sky and tinted the jagged peaks with a rutilant glow.

Slipping around to the back of the house, he found Joseph right where he expected—sitting at the kitchen table, a cup of coffee between his hands. Conner knocked, then gently pushed open a door he knew would be unlocked.

His heart warmed behind his ribs at the thought that some things don't ever change.

"Grandfather," he greeted with a rueful smile.

"My son. Come in." The old man's eyes lit with genuine joy. "This is a wonderful surprise. Have some coffee. There's plenty."

Conner knew there would be. A Kolheek could always come home again.

Shafts of light streamed into the kitchen as Conner sat across from his grandfather at the table.

"I have some things I need to say to you."

"Nothing needs to be said, Conner." Joseph reached out knurled fingers, his touch gentle on the back of his grandson's hand.

"Please," Conner insisted, "you have to let me speak my mind. My heart is heavy. It's been heavy for a very long time." His chin dipped momentarily. But before he spoke again, he leveled his eyes onto Joseph's. His grandfather deserved the respect of direct eye contact.

"I haven't been the kind of grandson you deserve."

Joseph rested his forearm on the edge of the tabletop. "You have always made me proud. You went out and boldly made your way in this world. You are successful. You are happy. That is all I ever wanted for you."

"But I haven't been happy, Grandfather."

The admission made Joseph go quiet.

Conner sighed. "How can a man be happy when he refuses to take responsibility for his own life? His own choices? When he insists on blaming someone else for his own inadequacies?"

Joseph looked about to speak, but Conner rushed ahead. "I've been blaming you, Grandfather. I blamed you for taking my father away from me."

"You were just a boy, Conner. A child trying to survive."

"But now I'm a man," he pointed out. "That excuse isn't viable any longer." After a moment he said, "I remember now. I was the one who came to you seeking help. Seeking shelter. From my father's reckless behavior. I want you to know that I realize you only acted out of your love for me. That you sent Father away because it was in my best interest.''

Sadness slackened Joseph's proud features. ''Your father had a good heart, Conner. He simply couldn't get over his grief for your mother. He tried to drown it and ended up killing himself.''

Conner understood that Joseph was speaking of the accident that took his father's life. Softly Conner asked, ''Had you not fought with Dad…had you not forced him to leave me with you, I would have been in that vehicle with him that night, wouldn't I?''

Deep sentiment glistened in the old man's eyes as he nodded silently.

The men sat in the companionable quiet, each lost in the past.

Finally Conner said, ''At first I felt tremendously guilty that I had you send him away. And after Dad was killed, that guilt became too much for me to bear, so I allowed myself to believe a warped sense of reality and I blamed you for everything.'' His throat swelled with emotion. ''Can you ever forgive me?''

''There is nothing to forgive, my son. I love you. I would have done anything for you.''

''I know that,'' Conner said, heartfelt honesty thickening his words. ''And I want you to know that I love you. That I'm grateful for all you've done for me over the years.''

He reached out and grasped his grandfather's forearm. Joseph did the same, and for a long moment they basked in the poignant emotion passing between them.

"I want you to know—"

It was clear to Conner that the depth of his grandfather's feelings made it difficult for the older man to speak.

"—that I did everything I could to make your father see that he should not lose the blessing that was his life because he was unable to save the life of another."

Conner's spine straightened. "That's what I tried to tell Mattie. Well, my words weren't quite as eloquent, but...in my own inept way, that's the message I meant to convey to her."

When Mattie's name was mentioned, Joseph's mouth pulled into a smile. "She is your peace."

Astonished, Conner leaned forward a fraction. "How did you know?" But even as he voiced the query, he realized his question didn't need an answer. His grandfather had always been astute about such things.

"As much as you think she has given you," Joseph said, "you, my son, have given to her, too. She's had a huge obstacle she's been trying to overcome. An obstacle she hadn't even seen was in her way. You have helped to illuminate her path. The two of you make great harmony together."

Conner scrubbed his hand over his jaw as he grimaced. "I'm not so sure she would agree with you." He shook his head. "Last night I attacked everything she holds dear. Her work, her life's devotion, her integrity, even her common sense. I think my words may have ruined any chance the two of us may have had together.''

''Nonsense, my son.'' His grandfather chuckled then. ''The Great Spirit Father knew what he was doing when he created us. He knew we would speak foolishly, act foolishly. That is why he created in each of us the immense ability to forgive.'' Joseph's gaze turned soft. ''All you can do, my son, is go to her and confess all that you feel in your heart.''

Mattie stared out at the calm lake surface, hoping and praying the serenity of this place would still the riot of emotion churning through her. She had so many feelings roiling inside.

She was happy that Brenda and Scotty were on their way to safety in another part of the country. Mattie had contacted a woman in Albuquerque who was willing to offer them a place to stay until Brenda could find a job and get on her feet. It was impossible not to be filled with a great satisfaction knowing she was able to give two people in need a safe harbor.

But try as she might to hold on to those good feelings after returning from the bus station, Mattie had lost her grip on them again and again through the long, lonely night. She'd tossed and turned, and finally thrown back the sheet to rise and pace the rambling B and B.

Wrapped in a thick wool blanket, she'd gone out on her deck to watch the sun rise over the mountain range. Usually the glorious colors of the dawn filled her with hope and optimism. But that hadn't happened this morning.

Desolation weighed her down like a mantle of

heavy, wet cement, so she'd gotten dressed and come to the lake in search of some quiet.

Turning away from Conner last night had been one of the hardest things she'd ever done in her life. Granted, he'd said some mean things to her. And his opinions of her, of her work, had hurt. Terribly.

Yet she had realized that he'd been deeply affected by Scotty's presence. The boy had obviously stirred up memories of Conner's own childhood. Mattie had witnessed all the anguish Conner had been reliving; however, she'd turned her back on him and walked away. Left him there by the banks of the lake to deal with his torment all alone.

Her only consolation had been that she'd had two other people waiting for her...people who needed and depended on her. And Conner, in his distressed state of mind, wouldn't have accepted her help anyway.

It seemed that fate was intent on shoving a wedge between them.

Conner.

She would never forget the velvet touch of his fingertips on her face. Never forget the sweet taste of his kiss. Never forget the way he'd made her body blaze with an amazing need.

As wonderful as all the physical sensations were, there were other things she wouldn't forget about him. The kindness and concern he'd showed her from their very first moments together. The way he'd so quickly offered a helping hand with the carriage house. He'd made her laugh. He'd made her think. He'd made her *live*.

Conner had made her see that she'd become so

wrapped up in her work with the abused that she just might be missing out on life. And as much as she hated to admit it, she feared he was right.

But changing her course now was impossible. Circumstances had forced her to choose a direction five long years ago, and as lonely as this road was, it was her destiny.

Oh, Lord above, but that thought filled her with a bleakness that seemed unbearable. Tears welled and trailed down her cheeks unchecked.

''Mattie.''

She started at the sound of Conner's voice. Smoothing fingers over her tearstained face, she turned her head.

''I've been looking for you everywhere.'' He came closer.

''Conner—'' She turned her head away, unwilling to let him see that she'd been sitting here crying. ''I'm not really up to any more arguments right now.'' The exhaustion of being up all night suddenly made itself felt.

''You're upset,'' he observed.

Before she even realized it, he was seated next to her, his hands enveloping hers.

''The woman and the boy? Are they okay? Did something happen to them?''

Mattie's gaze flew to his face. His concern over Brenda and Scotty was genuine. Even after he'd railed at her, after he'd questioned her good judgment in helping Brenda to get herself and her son out of town, he still expressed an open and frank apprehension for their safety.

She realized in that very instant just how much

she loved this man. He was like no one she'd ever met before. He intrigued her. Attracted her. Captivated her.

Her chest felt constricted, as if there were an invisible band around her that was being tightened, notch by excruciating notch.

"Did you ever reach a point in your life—" she was utterly amazed at how the words tumbled off her tongue before she could stop them "—where you wanted something so badly that it actually hurt, yet you knew you could never have it?"

For the longest time he didn't speak, just sat there studying her face. An awkwardness crept over Mattie. Surely he would think she'd lost her mind.

Softly he asked, "What is it, Mattie? What has you so upset?"

You, she wanted to admit. But how fruitless would that be? Hadn't she already decided that fate itself was against her? Hadn't she figured out long ago that her road into the future would be a lonely one?

Instead of answering his question, she said, "Don't worry. Brenda and Scotty are fine." She sighed, her gaze stretching out across the glassy lake. "I'm just feeling a little blue, is all. It happens once the B and B is empty. My pent-up stress needs release."

Leaves from the branches towering overhead fluttered through the chilly autumn air, landing helter-skelter around them.

"Poor Mattie," he said, his tone holding no hint of condescension. "You put so much effort into saving those who can't fend for themselves. But who is going to save you?"

She pulled her hands from his. "I don't need to be saved, Conner."

"Don't be angry with me," he said. "I sure didn't mean to make you angry. But I do have to disagree with you. Everyone needs saving every now and then. I know I did."

It was impossible for her to hide the surprise and bewilderment she felt.

"And you, Mattie," he continued, "are the person who saved me. You persuaded me to seek the truth. And I did."

He told her all that he'd learned about the images in his dream, about his childhood, about his misplaced blame.

"I went to see my grandfather this morning," he told her. "He forgave me. Our relationship is closer now than it's ever been. I have you to thank for that."

She didn't know how to respond.

"No one could have succeeded in getting me to go hunting for the truth but you." He reached out and took her hand again. "So you see, you really did save me."

He smiled, but she was feeling too overwhelmed to do more than simply look at him.

His voice was as soft and sensual as black velvet when he suggested, "Let me save you, Mattie. Let me take away all your loneliness."

An irrational fear welled up, straightened her spine, had her feeling the urge to flee. She tried to tug her hand free, but he held tight.

"You know that's not possible, Conner."

"You don't have to give up your own happiness for the sake of others," he told her.

Ire flared. "Do you know what you're asking? I tried to make you understand how important my work is. I can't give it up. Ever."

"That's not what I'm suggesting, Mattie," he said. "You're not listening to me. Or else I'm not being clear. I want to be with you. I want to help you in your cause. Sweetheart, I truly believe that everything happens for a purpose. You and I were brought together for a reason. This was meant to be. I had lessons that you helped me to learn. And you have lessons that I can help you learn."

"That sounds so esoteric."

His smile only widened. "Life is a mystery, Mattie. We're not meant to understand everything. You said so yourself. But if fate hands you a gift, you'd best accept it." He paused a moment. "I think fate is handing us the gift of each other. The question is…are we going to accept it?"

Adoration shone in his eyes, in his handsome face. She couldn't believe her ears. Couldn't believe her eyes. Was he really saying that he thought they should be together?

The hope and expectation emanating from him made her heart soar.

"B-but…but," she stammered, "I run a B and B in Vermont. You have a company to run in Boston. How on earth—"

He laughed then, cupping both her hands in his and lifting them to his lips. His mouth felt warm against her flesh.

"Honey, those minor details will take care of

themselves," he told her. "I'll be more than happy to start over again. I'm that confident in my belief that you and I are meant to be together."

He was sure enough for both of them, and that just took her breath away.

"Oh, Conner," she whispered, "I think I've been in love with you all of my life."

His mesmerizing onyx eyes searched her face as his hand tenderly cradled her jaw.

"And I've loved you forever, too, Mattie." He kissed her then, his mouth hot and deliciously possessive. "Forever."

Epilogue

Mattie's nerves were jangling like a dozen bells as she turned to face her friends Gwen and Lori and waited for their verdict.

"You're beautiful," Lori breathed. Happy tears sprang to her eyes, and Mattie had to smile at her friend's emotional state. Lori's very pregnant body was a deluge of rampant hormones—that much was evident.

"You are beautiful, Mattie," Gwen agreed. "That outfit is just gorgeous."

When Conner had told Mattie that the ceremonial robe his mother had worn at her own wedding ceremony was in storage and offered it to Mattie to wear at their nuptials, Mattie hadn't been able to say yes fast enough.

The doeskin robe was supple as a whisper. The bodice of the dress was covered with tiny cylindrical shells that had been polished to a high sheen. A sash gathered the soft hide fabric just beneath her breasts, with what seemed a thousand narrow strips falling from the midriff over the skirt so that each step she took caused a sea of movement around her legs. The hem struck her midcalf, a length that accentuated the white beaded moccasins adorning her feet.

A Kolheek hairdresser on the rez had agreed to style Mattie's hair in traditional fashion. Her flaxen tresses were parted on an angle and plaited into two fat braids, one falling over each shoulder. Petite freshwater pearls had been intertwined into the full length of each braid.

"You don't think it's too much?" Mattie asked.

"You look like a golden goddess," Lori said.

Gwen added, "An Indian princess. Conner is going to be amazed."

Lori sniffed and dabbed her nose with a tissue. "A Christmas Eve wedding. Could there be anything more romantic?"

"Stop that crying," Mattie told her friend, "or you're going to have me blubbering like a baby."

"Don't you dare." Gwen wagged her finger at Mattie. "You don't want your mascara to run."

There was a knock on the door, and Grey poked his head into the room. "It's time," he told them all. When he saw his wife's tears, he hurried to her and wrapped her in his arms, kissed her gently on the temple. "Hey, sweetie, are you okay?"

"I'm fine." Lori sniffed. "I'm just happy for Mattie and Conner, is all."

The sound of ceremonial drums filled the air. Grey looked at each woman in turn. "It's show time. The whole tribe is out there."

"Grey!" Mattie's insides quivered. "Don't remind me. I'm nervous enough as it is."

When Conner and Mattie had gone to Joseph to ask him to perform a traditional Kolheek marriage ceremony for them, the elderly shaman had asked if they'd consider allowing the entire community the opportunity to attend. Mattie had been happy to share her special day with the residents of the reservation, but now the thought of walking out there in front of all those people made her feel weak in the knees.

She made her way down the hallway of the community center, a huge smile spreading over her face when she met her parents. She kissed both her mother and her father.

"You ready?" her father asked.

Mattie nodded, too emotional to speak.

Clearly her mother was choked up, too, so rather than say a word the woman simply handed her daughter a small spray of colorful wildflowers.

Flanked by her loving parents, Mattie held her head high as she entered the large domed arena. A hush fell over the crowd, the only sound the intense beating of the drums.

Joseph wore his full ceremonial regalia, complete with an elaborate headdress covered with eagle feathers.

Then Mattie saw him.

Conner.

Her heart pounded more fiercely than the rhythm of the drums, her blood churning with excitement. She couldn't believe she would soon be Mrs. Conner Thunder.

He looked so handsome. His sleeveless, tan-colored tunic drew attention to his muscular arms. Fringed leggings hugged his powerful thighs. His long hair hung loose, and a strip of colorful, hand-woven fabric was tied around his head.

But it was his gaze that stole her breath away. Those onyx eyes of his communicated the delicious promise of all the passion he intended to shower on her...soon. Very soon.

The love that filled her heart was reflected in her smile as she went to meet the love of her life.

Later that night, with their clothing tossed hither and yon, with the last vestiges of romantic candle-light flickering and sputtering in the darkness, they lay together, bare flesh to bare flesh. Mattie had never experienced such glorious satiation.

Conner raised himself up on one elbow, his face only inches from hers. He kissed the tip of her nose, his fingers tracing down the length of her throat, over the delicate and oh-so-sensitive curve of her breast. Her body once again quickened in response to his hungry touch.

"Are you sorry we didn't go someplace exotic for our honeymoon?" he asked. "Bermuda? Cancún?"

She shook her head, her white-gold hair spread about her. "There's no place more beautiful than New England in the winter."

"But it's *cold*."

The chuckle that bubbled from her throat couldn't be described as anything but purely carnal. "It's also the perfect excuse for us to stay right here...under the covers."

Conner's grin was sexy as all get-out. "There is that."

His kiss left her breathless with need. She snaked her hand down beneath the sheets, smoothing her fingertips over his firm buttocks, pressing herself against him wantonly. He countered with a desirous growl that made her giggle.

Then she sobered. "Conner, do you really believe we were made for each other? That we're truly soul mates?"

"With all my heart I do," he said.

Then he set about proving it to her.

* * * * *

SILHOUETTE *Romance*®

THE THUNDER CLAN

A family of proud, passionate people!

You've read brothers Nathan's and Grey's stories...
now read about their cousin, brooding black-sheep-by-
choice Conner, in THUNDER IN THE NIGHT (SR #1647),
coming in February 2003, only from
Donna Clayton and Silhouette Romance!

Nathan's story:
THE SHERIFF'S 6-YEAR-OLD SECRET
(SR #1623)

Grey's story:
THE DOCTOR'S PREGNANT PROPOSAL
(SR #1635)

Conner's story:
THUNDER IN THE NIGHT
(SR #1647)

Available at your favorite retail outlet.

Silhouette®
Where love comes alive™

If you enjoyed what you just read,
then we've got an offer you can't resist!

Take 2 bestselling love stories FREE!

Plus get a FREE surprise gift!

COMING NEXT MONTH

#1648 HER SECRET CHILDREN—Judith McWilliams

How could a woman who'd never been pregnant have twins living in England? Vicky Sutton was determined to discover just who had stolen her eggs—but never expected to meet James Thayer, father of the twins and a man afraid of parenthood! Would this twosome become a foursome?

#1649 PROTECTING THE PRINCESS—Patricia Forsythe

American security expert Reeve Stratton came to Inbourg to guard the beautiful and stubborn Princess Anya and her young son. But close quarters with the enchanting princess was leading to some very unprofessional ideas…and to a few stolen kisses….

#1650 THE TYCOON'S DOUBLE TROUBLE—Susan Meier
Daycare Dads

Policewoman Sadie Evans's temporary job of baby-sitting billionaire Troy Cramer's wayward twins was throwing her life in an uproar. Still, it was hard to resist a man with blue eyes, broad shoulders and a need for her that went beyond what either of them expected….

#1651 KISS ME, KAITLYN—Cynthia Rutledge

Aspiring designer Kaitlyn Killeen could not afford to fall in love with rugged Clay McCashlin—no matter how breathless he made her feel! But the handsome rebel had a hidden agenda—and identity. Soon Kaitlyn had to choose between the career she'd always wanted, and the enigmatic man who left her wanting more!

#1652 IN THE SHEIKH'S ARMS—Sue Swift

During a morning ride, the independent Cami Ellison met Rayhan ibn-Malik, her mysterious and handsome neighbor. Caught up in his passionate kisses, she became his bride—not realizing revenge was in his heart. But would Ray's plan to whisk the young beauty away to a foreign land prove that *love*—not vengeance—was his motivation?

#1653 A DAY LATE AND A BRIDE SHORT—Holly Jacobs

Attorney Elias Donovan needed a wife in order to be considered for partnership in his firm. What he ended up with was fiancée-of-convenience Sarah Madison. Soon Sarah found herself planning her own elaborate fake wedding! But would their time together lead to real marriage?

SRCNM0203